Then he nodded soberly and said, "We'd have heard if they'd been busting through any heavy doors in the recent past."

Longarm muttered, "I wish you'd quit telling me things I already know and let me listen for *them* right now, dammit!"

So Vail shut up and the two of them waited on the stairwell with their sixguns as the raw, wet winds rattled the unbolted door they were covering. Vail wanted to say he couldn't see how they'd ever hear cautious footsteps above all that moaning and pattering outside. But he knew his senior deputy had keener ears and seemed to be listening with that tight coiled stillness of a store cat by a mouse hole.

But the two of them stood ready on the stairs for a million years, and when something finally happened, it happened without warning.

A heap of gunfights start that way.

TABOR EVANS

LONGARM

AND THE DEVIL'S SISTER

JOVE BOOKS, NEW YORK

LONGARM AND THE DEVIL'S SISTER

A Jove Book / published by arrangement with
the author

PRINTING HISTORY
Jove edition / April 1999

The Penguin Putnam Inc. World Wide Web site address is
http://www.penguinputnam.com

ISBN: 0-515-12485-0

A JOVE BOOK®
Jove Books are published by The Berkley Publishing Group,
a member of Penguin Putnam Inc.,
375 Hudson Street, New York, New York 10014.
JOVE and the "J" design
are trademarks belonging to Jove Publications, Inc.

PRINTED IN THE UNITED STATES OF AMERICA

10 9 8 7 6 5 4 3 2 1

LONGARM

AND THE
DEVIL'S SISTER

Chapter 1

U.S. Deputy Marshal Custis Long of the Denver District Court was neither the arresting officer nor a material witness at the trial of David Deveruex. So Longarm, as he was better known around the federal building, might not have spent so much time in the courtroom down the hall from his own office if it hadn't been for golden curls, a Mona Lisa smile, and a well-turned ankle.

Devil Dave Deveruex, as he was better known along the Owlhoot trail, had greasy black hair, a perpetual sneer, and you couldn't make out his ankles because of his high-priced Justin boots. His trial for Murder in the First had been strung out beyond all human reason by the squad of high-priced lawyers his well-heeled Texas kin had hired to defend the offensive young runt. But Longarm didn't care.

The golden curls, Mona Lisa smile, well-turned ankle, and other nice things about her belonged to Court Recorderess Elsbeth Flagg, who had recently transferred down from Cheyenne and hadn't made too many friends around Denver so far.

It was Longarm's hope that once the pretty little thing got used to seeing his face around the federal building it might be safe to ask her if she'd like to watch the sun go down behind the Front Range from the statehouse steps or, better yet, from a buggy parked out to Cherry Hill.

Neither offer would have sounded tempting that Thursday morning in March, because it was a raw, wet windy day outside and they still had all Friday and half of Saturday to work with. Longarm figured, at the rate things were finally starting to move, Judge Dickerson would charge the jury Friday morning and sentence Devil Dave on Saturday, giving the mean little shit at least one Sabbath to reflect on his mad-dog ways. But what if Miss Elsbeth didn't recognize him when he moved to join her at the conclusion of this tedious trial, when everyody who hadn't been condemned to death would be in good spirits because it was over at last?

Deputy Gilfoyle, a young cuss of some charm, had tried in vain to just help the blonde court recorderess with all those legal pads and such she had to tote back and forth from her own office across the hall, and had been frozen in his tracks by that withering look Queen Victoria and other ladies of quality reserved for dog shit and uppity hired help. The trial had dragged on for nigh two weeks and Longarm had been sitting in her line of fire on those rare occasions she'd raised her big blue eyes from her shorthand notes. But he couldn't say whether she'd been looking at him or sort of through him as she just rested her eyes. He'd tried smiling at her a couple of times or more. He couldn't tell whether she'd smiled back or not. That faint ghost of a smile on a cool, if not downright prim pair of lips, had made those prints of Mona Lisa popular in many a trail-town saloon, as they encouraged wistful arguments along the bar. For, depending on how a man studied that expression and how much he'd had to drink, Miss Mona Lisa could be fixing to tell everyone to just go away and leave her alone, or fixing to invite one and all to just drop their damned pants and get in line.

A gust of wind rattled the rain-lashed windows and one of the defense lawyers rose in the silence that followed to croak like a frog about a motion Longarm couldn't follow. The defense team had been forced to pass on logic some time

2

back, as witness after witness put Devil Dave in that bank with a ten-gauge scattergun while refusing to believe the bank vault had a time-lock as those terrified victims had tried to tell him.

The fair but firm presiding Judge Dickerson must have been as weary of senseless motions as Longarm, by then. He banged his gavel and told the lawyer to shut up and sit down as the weary-eyed blonde recording the exchange favored the iron-haired judge with a grateful smile. It was going on noon and it looked as if the judge was about to adjourn for the dinner hour when all hell busted loose.

Longarm had run off to war as a schoolboy and lived through many a gunfight since by never standing tall and staring about like a big-ass bird while he figured out where shots were being fired from. So he hit the courtroom floor and rolled under a heavy oak table between him and the recording blonde as he drew the double-action Colt .44–40 he carried cross-draw under the coat of his tobacco tweed suit. He lost his pancaked coffee-brown Stetson along the way as he rolled on toward Elsbeth Flagg on the far side. He saw to his relief that she'd already hit the floor on her own to sprawl face down amid her scattered pads and pencils.

Then he saw how still she lay as he gently took her by one shoulder to let her know he was there. It would have been pointless to say much with that gunfire going on all around.

Then the fusillade stopped as suddenly as it had begun, to be replaced by screaming, moaning, and groaning amid the swirling clouds of gunsmoke filling the courtroom from waist-high to the ceiling.

Somebody yelled at the bailiff to fling open some damned windows. It sounded a lot like Judge Dickerson.

Longarm shook the prone blonde for attention and warned, "Stay down. I'll see if I can figure things out better!"

He rose gingerly between the massive table and the judge's shellacked oak bar to find that once he was standing tall he couldn't see shit in all that smoke. He dropped down to one knee, where he could get a better look at Elsbeth Flagg. He didn't like what he could see. The stain in the back of her dark blue bodice looked darker than blood usually seeped from a bullet hole. But the dyes of her new dress were likely bleeding some, too.

"Miss Elsbeth?" Longarm quietly but urgently asked as he took her by the shoulder some more.

She didn't answer. When he moved her fine-boned head enough to see her pretty face, her big blue eyes were open and she still wore that Mona Lisa smile on her pretty lips. She was dead as a turd in a milk bucket. He could only hope she'd never known what hit her.

He sprang back to his considerable full height, growling low in his throat as he closed in on the defense table through the smoke, letting his gun muzzle lead the way. But when he got there, the smoke now just a tad thinner, he saw one of Devil Dave's lawyers sprawled face down across that table. Two witnesses were down as well. One looked dead. The other was clutching his chest and babbling like a brook about double crosses as bloody foam bubbled out of his nose and mouth.

"What in the fuck is going on!" thundered Judge Dickerson in all his majesty from somewhere in the noisy fog. Another voice Longarm recognized as the bailiff's plaintively replied, "There was three of them. They looked like Mexicans. They was standing in the rear against the wall when they suddenly whupped out their guns and commenced to empty the same into everybody! We have Lord knows how many dead and dying in here at the moment, Your Honor!"

The judge roared, "I could see that much brewing up before the smoke got so thick! I meant how come, and what about the infernal accused?"

A deputy bailiff called out from another corner, "I fear Devil Dave has escaped on us, Your Honor! This exit here stands wide open now. It was supposed to be shut and barred!"

The judge commenced to call down the wrath of Jehovah on one and all as Longarm, not having the time to take it all

4

in, was already out the same exit and running down the service stairs that led, he knew, to the doors leading out to the ground floor or basement, with neither open to the public as a rule.

He got to the first story door, tried it, and found it locked, as it was supposed to be, with a damned murder trial going on upstairs.

He found the door leading into the basement locked as well. So the prisoner hadn't escaped into the file rooms and such beyond.

That left the sub basement or no-shit cellar where the coal bins, furnace room, and such were never supposed to be entered by anyone but the janitorial staff. Longarm wasn't sure how many other exits there'd be and he wasn't looking forward to meeting up with anyone as mad-dog mean as Devil Dave and who knew how many henchmen in a dark cellar! But he tried the latch anyway.

He found it locked. The murderous little shit hadn't escaped by that route. The courtroom exit had simply been flung open by accident or as what stage magicians and con men knew as "misdirection".

"It worked." Longarm growled as he had to charge up two flights of steps, cussing himself for a fool, even though he understood how such misdirections worked.

The pretty stage magician who'd explained some tricks of her trade to him, in bed, one friendly time, had confided how magicians hated to perform in front of small children or lunatics because they, and they alone, let their attention and eyes wander aimless whilst the magician was trying to make them watch his right hand instead of his left hand.

When you misdirected right you got natural folk to look in the most logical direction. A lawman in hot pursuit who hadn't chased down a stairwell behind a flung-open exit door would have had to be sort of thick or childish. But as he stepped back into the courtroom, now a more horrible scene with that smoke cleared out, he wistfully wished an armed and dangerous half-wit had chased Devil Dave in a less sen-

5

sible way. For, try as he might as he stood there staring about in dismay at the dead and wounded in the shot-up courtroom, Longarm still had no idea which way the prisoner and those three or more confederates had moved amid all that smoke and confusion!

As if to prove his point, the main door to the outside corridor was flung wide to admit a trio of uniformed guards and Longarm's own boss from down the hall, U.S. Marshal William Vail.

One of the guards declared, "Nobody saw them leave by any of the regular exits downstairs, Your Honor! That still leaves a mess of first story windows, and they could have rolled over many a sill, in many an unoccupied office!"

"I want the whole neighborhood canvassed for witnesses!" His Honor roared, adding, "Somebody should have noticed grown men jumping out of windows in broad-ass daylight!"

The somewhat younger and stockier Billy Vail called back, "Got my deputies out tending to that chore already, Your Honor and, no offense, it ain't exactly broad day outside. It's raining fire and salt. So the streets would have been clearer than usual just now. I have another team of deputies searching the building, even as we speak. If they're still on the premises, they're good as caught!"

Then Vail spotted Longarm in the crowd and grumped over to him on his stubbier legs, saying, "*Bueno!* I admire a deputy who don't need to be told. What's the story on yonder stairs to the basement?"

Longarm holstered his .44–40 as he replied, "*Nada.* Blind gut. Locked doors barring escape down yonder."

Vail was younger than the judge but older and more experienced than his senior deputy. He proved this when he asked Longarm, "What about up yonder? That stairwell opens to the roof. So do all the others in this fair-sized building when you study on it!"

Longarm drew his sixgun again as he whirled on one heel to retrace his own steps, muttering, "I wasn't studying. I was

6

chasing 'em the way a kitten chases a string, and I ought to be roped and branded for a greenhorn!''

His boss drew his own sidearm to tag along, declaring, "The other doors at this end of the courtroom lead to the holding cells and the judge's chambers. I have Smiley and Dutch covering the hall exit from the judge's chambers. But the rascal who planned this bust-out had to know this building better than most!"

Longarm headed up the stairwell, sniffing the damp air as he called back, "The prisoner had no way of exploring on his own, betwixt times the court was in session. Must have been one of the three or more the bailiff described as Mexican. I never looked their way before the whole place was too smoked-up to see shit. The only one I can be sure of on sight is Devil Dave Deveruex in the vanished flesh."

Taking the steps two at a time he tried the door on the next landing with his free hand. It was locked. He kept going, adding, "All I know about Devil Dave is that they were fixing to find him guilty for that murderous holdup down by Pike's Peak. But he looks sort of Mex, talks sort of Tex, and they say he went bad under the Reconstruction, down West Texas way."

Vail puffed up the stairs after Longarm, gasping, "As a matter of record he's Irish-Mex. His daddy served on the Mexican side with the San Patricio brigade back in '47 before he married up with a Spanish land grant on the Pecos that both sides agreed to recognize under the peace terms that followed. How come I'm telling you all this, seeing you've been attending his trial and, come to study on it, who ordered you to attend his trial, old son?"

Longarm tried another door, found it locked as well and forged onward and upward without answering. Vail waited until they stood side by side at the head of the stairs and he could breathe again before he shot his senior deputy a knowing look and asked, "Is that why we're so pissed off about that dead blonde down yonder, old son?"

To which Longarm felt obliged to reply, "You have my

7

word, as a man, that Miss Elsbeth never gave this saddle tramp one lick of encouragement. Take a look at this barrel bolt.''

Vail did. They both knew nobody worried about burglars landing out on the big flat roof in a hot air balloon. But the fickle winds off the Front Range over to the west could blow serious in most any weather and so the doors leading out on the roof were kept bolted on the inside as a rule.

Vail started to shove past. But Longarm said, "Don't. We've had our differences, Billy Vail, but I'd just hate to have to be the one to tell your old woman you died from a bad case of the stupids!''

Vail allowed himself to be herded a few steps down, but he still protested. "I meant to fling the door wide and crab to one side as I tore out, old son. But to tell the pure truth they've likely run down another flight by this time!''

Longarm grimly answered, "How? All the other stairwells leading up to the roof are barred from the inside, like this one was before they opened it just now!''

Vail started to say something dumb. Then he nodded soberly and said, "We'd have heard if they'd been busting through any heavy doors in the recent past.''

Longarm muttered, "I wish you'd quit telling me things I already know and let me listen for *them* right now dammit!''

So Vail shut up and the two of them waited on the stairwell with their sixguns as the raw, wet winds rattled the unbolted door they were covering. Vail wanted to say he couldn't see how they'd ever hear cautious footsteps above all that moaning and pattering outside. But he knew his senior deputy had keener ears and seemed to be listeing with that tight coiled stillness of a store cat crouched by a mouse hole.

But the two of them stood ready on the stairs for a million years, and when something finally happened, it happened without warning.

A heap of gunfights started that way.

Chapter 2

As old soldiers knew the hard way, you got to be an old soldier by pussyfooting on patrol and charging all-out when they might know you were coming. So the gunslick who'd trapped himself atop the rain swept roof retraced his steps with a vengeance and a Schofield .45 in each fist as he kicked the door in, saw he was not alone at the head of the stairs, and went down noisy, with four sixguns blazing in homicidal intent.

The obvious border Mex in a soaked-through *charro* outfit blew Billy Vail's hat off with one wild round and plucked at Longarm's coat tails with another as he gathered three rounds of more sincerely aimed .44–40 to his breast and fell back out the door to stare up into the falling rain with a sheepish little smile.

Longarm snapped, "Cover me!" as he dashed through their gunsmoke, out the door and across the wet gravel-covered roofing tar to hunker behind the dubious shelter of a skylight frame. When nobody pegged a shot at either of them, Billy Vail broke cover to leapfrog beyond Longarm as far as another shedlike exit to the roof above another stairwell. And so it went until they'd worked their way to the far end to discover they had the whole soggy expanse to their soaking selves.

9

Down below, the streets of Downtown Denver seemed filled with wet faces staring up at them through the rain. A meat wagon from County General had just reined in by a side entrance with the hides of its team steaming. Billy Vail suggested they get back inside before they wound up in the hospital their ownselves. Longarm glanced off to the west, where the nearby Front Range was lost to view in the shimmering silver curtains of the gullywasher as he wistfully wondered how the late Elsbeth Flagg might have responded to an invite to a sunset view in dryer weather. As he followed Billy Vail over the Mexican sprawled half in and half out of the doorway they'd dashed out of, he quietly said, "I want the rest of 'em, Billy. I got personal reasons."

Vail had hunkered by the body in the rain and started going through the pockets of the Mex rider's *charro* outfit as he quietly replied, "I saw her laid out on the floor downstairs, old son. They nailed at least half a dozen others in that wild fusillade and some of them have to be as dead or dying. So I don't see how we could get out of tracking the bastards, serious, whether we wanted to or not. Judge Dickerson was sure pissed off about all this."

Vail found a wallet and opened the wet leather to add, "I seem to owe Old Mexico an apology. This murderous cocksucker wasn't no fucking greaser. He was a fucking Indian. A Mimbres off the San Carlos Agency, according to this ration card from the Bureau of Indian Affairs."

Longarm stared soberly down at the man they'd killed as he quietly said, "Ain't no such thing as a Mimbres from the San Carlos Agency, no matter what the BIA tries to tell 'em. I reckon only a Mimbres could explain why this is so, but when Washington decided to consolidate all the so-called Apache at San Carlos in '75 the Mimbres who liked things better around Ojo Caliente, well east of Apache Pass, allowed they'd as soon stay put."

Vail got up to step inside, still waving the dead man's ID as he demanded, "How come this here late Ramon Kayitah

10

was registered as a Mimbres with the San Carlos Agency if he wouldn't live there?''

Longarm stepped in out of the rain as well, dryly observing, ''He wasn't living there. We just now killed him in Denver. Victorio is off the San Carlos Agency this spring with his own Mimbres and a whole lot of pissed-off Mescalero from New Mexico as well. The BIA resettled some few Mountain Apache or NaDéné over in the Arizona Desert, as long as they had young Johnny Clum as an agent they could get along with. Sort of. Since Clum was forced out by sterner politicos who found him too flexible, they've had a tougher time controlling NaDéné. That's what Washington calls it when they get to pick the color of your shit and tell you where to shit it. Controlling.''

Vail found his wet hat on the stairs and bent to pick it up and put it back on as he decided, ''Well, nobody had the late Ramon Kayitah all that controlled and for all we know the others could have been Indians as well. I keep telling you children not to leap at conclusions. But I just did it my ownself, knowing Devil Dave Deveruex was half Mex from the Pecos Valley and assuming his pals were from down home.''

Longarm followed him down ‘a stairwell still reeking of gunsmoke as he reloaded along the way, observing, ''You could be doing it some more, no offense. One full-blood running with *mestizo vaqueros* works as well as an Irish-Mex off a Tex-Mex land grant running with a whole tribe of Indians. There's this Denver bakery I stop by on the way home, now and again, owned and operated by full-blooded Arapaho. The name they're going by, these days, would be Plimmons. They didn't have to move to the east with the more feathersome Arapaho in '75 because they chose to be self-supporting and law-abiding residents of this here state capital.''

Vail snorted, ''Are you saying that son of a bitch we just had to gun down like a mad dog could be defined as law-abiding?''

Longarm shrugged and answered, simply, ''We both accepted him as a Tex-Mex rider until he lay dead on the roof,

11

didn't we? My point is that there's more than one way to leave an Indian reserve. For every Victorio or even Chief Joseph there must be a dozen disgusted Indians who just get a haircut, dress up more natural, and find something else to do. Like baking bread, herding cows, or riding the owlhoot trail with other outlaws of uncertain ancestry.''

Vail led the way back into Judge Dickerson's cleared court, where a smell of gunsmoke and spilled gore still lingered as the last of the bodies were being carried out.

His Honor came toward them, still wearing his black cotton robes and the expression of a man who'd just caught his wife in bed with a hired hand. Before Vail could tell him they'd nailed at least one of the gang, His Honor roared, ''Why are you both fucking the dog here at the scene of the crime? The bastards are long gone! Why haven't you gone after them?''

Vail growled, ''We just come down from gunning the one who run up on the roof. What was Your Honor thinking of when them three gun-toting strangers entered his courtroom all dressed up like border *buscaderos*? Weren't you fixing to sentence Devil Dave to any time at all?''

The iron-gray hanging judge declared, ''All right. There's blame to go around, and you say you got at least one of them, Billy?''

Vail smiled modestly and confessed, ''Longarm, here, put just as many rounds in him. His name was Ramon Kayitah. Assimilated Mimbres Apache, living white. Living Mex, least ways. We're still working on who or what the other two might have been. Their *charro* riding outfits and *buscadero* gun rigs fit the escaped prisoner's home range in the lower reaches of the Pecos Valley. We now know that Frank and Jesse James lit out for Clay County and their Missouri kith and kin when that Northfield raid went sour on them, so . . .''

Longarm pointed out. ''Frank and Jesse rode west into the Dakota Territory when they ran into all that trouble in Minnesota.''

Vail shrugged and said, ''Whatever. The point is that Frank and Jesse finally wound up back home with their momma and

12

we know Dave Deveruex grew up on a land grant his own widowed momma still grazes a swamping herd on, with a shithouse full of Tex-Mex help a growing boy with Tex-Mex features could blend into pretty good. So just in case we fail to find him and his other pals holed up here in Denver I mean to wire a ranger captain I used to ride with before the war and . . .''

"I wish you wouldn't.'' Longarm cut in.

The two older men stared at Longarm as if they suspected him of farting in church. Billy Vail said, "I thought you just told me you had a personal hard-on for Devil Dave Deveruex, old son.''

Longarm said, "I do. That's why I want to catch him instead of making him look bright-eyed and bushy-tailed to his Tex-Mex admiration society. Lawmen private and public have tried in vain to cut the trails of Frank and Jesse within a day's ride of their known home address. In '75 the Pinkertons lobbed a fire bomb through their momma's window and only managed to cripple her and kill their nine-year-old half-brother, Archie Samuels.''

He let that sink in before he added, "Their unwanted kin were sitting there like trusting lambs because neither Frank nor Jesse were home at the time. They've never been home when the law comes calling because no lawman can ride a furlong into Clay County without some kissing cousin letting Frank and Jesse know the law's riding in. The Texas Rangers have to know Devil Dave hails from that land grant in the Lower Pecos Valley, don't they?''

Vail nodded and said, "Well sure they do. How did you think we knew that much about him? The mean little cuss commenced his wild career by shooting a colored cavalry trooper during the Reconstruction. The kid allowed the Good Lord had never created horses to be rode by Ethiopians. Nobody in West Texas was talking to the state police imposed on them by the Reconstruction. So Devil Dave's next victim was a white carpetbagger the Good Lord had endowed with

13

a money belt, a diamond stick pin, and a gold watch. But that was then and this is now.''

Judge Dickerson made a wry face as he nodded reluctantly and said, ''President Hayes in his infinite wisdom ended the last vestiges of the Reconstruction back in '77, and, as soon as those Texas rebs were back in the saddle, they disbanded those state troopers and brought back those dad-blamed rowdy rangers!''

Then he remembered who he was talking to and quicky assured Billy Vail he was only referring to those Texas Rangers who'd ridden for the Confederacy, after the times young Ranger Vail had ridden under Captain Big Foot Wallace.

Vail was explaining how other Scotchmen had called Big Foot Wallace ''Sandy'' when Longarm cut in to steer them back on more recent trails by saying, ''My point is that nobody's ever been able to throw down on Devil Dave Deveruex or find a soul who's ever heard of him on or about his own home range. If we know this, he knows this. If he makes it out of Colorado, no matter where else he may circle, he's likely to wind up along the Lower Pecos, sooner or later.''

Vail and the judge exchanged glances. Vail turned back to his senior deputy to patiently but firmly demand, ''Make up your mind. I just now said I could wire the rangers down yonder and you asked me not to because you want Deveruex and them two other killers caught? What am I missing here?''

Longarm said, ''The best way to catch him. Neither you nor me nor a company of rangers backed by a squadron of cavalry would ever cut that local hero's trail in his own neck of the chaparral. But it's going on market-herding time in Texas. It's a logical time for an out-of-work cowhand to drift in, looking for work, and I can still rope and throw if I have to.''

Judge Dickerson grinned wolfishly and said, ''By jimmies I'll write you a federal warrant that ought to stand up in Old Mexico. It can't be lawful anywhere to shoot up a courtroom while a trial's in progress!''

Vail knew West Texas better. He frowned dubiously and

said, "I'll go along with it if you'll take Smiley and Dutch along with you. Lord knows they both look more like saddle tramps than our current civil service dress code allows, and Smiley might pass for a Mex at drygulch distance, being part Pawneee and all."

Longarm shook his head and said, "That would be dumb, no offense. Anybody can see that no lawman would ride in alone if he had one lick of sense. As soon as I look like I have somebody covering my back I commence to look suspicious. After that I'd as soon work alone and not have to worry about covering anyone else's back."

"It's too big a boo. You ain't riding into that nest of vipers all alone!" said Billy Vail, as if he meant it.

Then young Henry, the squirt who played the typewriter in their office down the hall, came in with the blue-uniformed Sergeant Nolan of Denver P.D.

Henry said, "Deputy Gilfoyle just reported in from a quick canvas of the neighborhood. The rain had swept the streets clear until we had all that gunplay. A swamper at the Parthenon Saloon stepped out into their back alley, got wet without seeing anything, and stepped back in the doorway just as three men came arunning. Swamper makes it two Mex riders in *charro* outfits and a dapper young gent in a suit but no hat."

"That was them." Billy Vail decided, adding, "Which way did they go?"

Henry said, "The swamper can't say. He ducked inside entire as soon as one of the *vaqueros* slapped leather and cussed at him."

Sergeant Nolan consulted the notebook he was holding in one hamlike fist as he volunteered, "One of your lads made it over to our precinct house with the news of the breakout a tad too late. We'd been keeping an eye on three unusually prosperous Mexican strangers in town. Our watch commander's sent a detail to the rooming house they were staying in near the Union Station. We're going to be as surprised as the rest of you if they haven't checked out

15

without leaving any forwarding address. I knew them three were up to no good, what with their fancy Mex outfits and no visible means of support. But every time we arrest some stranger on suspicion of vagrancy we catch hell from the Magistrate's Court if they can show the judge two dollars or more in cash.''

Another copper badge in blue came in to report to Sergeant Nolan on their suspicious strangers. Longarm and the others listened as Denver P.D. exclaimed, "They were long gone when we got to that boarding house, but we may have cut their trail. According to the landlady, one of the Mexicans she recalls as Ramon told her they had a train to catch, so he wanted her to give him back some room rent he'd advanced her. She told him hell would freeze over first and then their leader, a gent she recalls as a Mister Hogan in spite of his Mex features, cussed at Ramon in Spanish, told her to keep the money, and the three of them lit out. She thought they were running for that train in the rain. We sent Ryan over to the depot in the unlikely event it was three other Mexicans shooting things up over here at the federal building.''

As if to prove his point two more copper badges trudged in, soaked to the skin in soggy boots. The one who had to be Ryan gasped, "Jesus, Mary, and Joseph, it's a grand day for the ducks and we just missed the murtherous *trinear* by a *falt go leth*! They told us at the *stesean* that two greasers and a white boy boarded the Burlington express north to Cheyenne and the cross-country Union Pacific and all and all!''

Nolan said he'd wire Cheyenne P.D. Ryan said he already had. Longarm said, "We proved up on the roof that the one called Ramon was sort of dumb. Neither Devil Dave nor the smoother *vaquero* called Hogan are as apt to run into a likely trap. They'll get off somewhere betwixt here and Cheyenne and go to ground in some hideout they've had plenty of time to set up. So don't that give me time to make it to West Texas a spell before they get there themselves? I mean, if I managed

16

to be taken as a harmless drifter who was already there instead of riding in after them . . .''

Billy Vail cut in to say, "I know what you mean. It's worth a try. But you're sure as shit bucking the odds, you stubborn young cuss!''

Chapter 3

The late Ramon Kayitah had proven on the roof that rushing ahead thoughtless could take as much as fifty years off a man's life. Hence, even though old Billy Vail could be a mother hen to his deputies, his orders to do some homework on Devil Dave Deveruex before he tried to beat him to his own back door made a heap of sense.

Longarm hadn't been taking notes as he'd sat closer to the late Elsbeth Flagg, watching *her* take notes. So it made him feel sort of odd as he sat in the judge's chambers after closing time, going over a dead gal's transcribed and typed-up court records by lamplight as the wind and rain kept trying to open the windows to the dark outside.

The bare facts of Devil Dave's most recent outburst down by Pike's Peak only told him that the young Tex-Mex was a mad dog with an itchy trigger finger. It didn't prove he was good or bad in a gunfight. Most any sort of gun-hand could blow away bank tellers or innocent bystanders who weren't fighting back.

The longer yellow sheets, or criminal record, of the mean squirt took up a heap more paper than the transcripts of his unfinished trial. It was impossible to tell whether that poor gal they'd killed out yonder in the courtroom had typed the earlier transcripts. All court records were worded in that same sedate way, without a lick of emotion as they described such earlier misdeeds as gunning a town drunk, just to see how long it would take anyone to notice he lay dead instead of drunk in a gutter. Longarm knew the dead gal had read that, whether she'd typed it or not. He wondered how she'd felt about the prisoner as she'd sat there recording his trial, looking cool as a cucumber, and now she lay down at the morgue on a cold zinc table, and if they didn't pump some formalin in her veins and stick a cannula up her ass to drain her guts, she was fixing to look just awful before they could get her home for her kin to bury.

He leafed through the yellow sheets to where they began with the one son of an otherwise respected family gunning that colored trooper and then bragging about it. Other offenses followed, one right after another, with none of them making financial sense. From the bare-bones background offered in old warrants and arrest records Longarm had the Deveruex y Lopez clan of Val Verde, Terrell, and Crocket County, Texas, owning many a cow, grazing many an acre under a modest army of hired help ruled by the widow of the late Sean Deveruex and managed by the older daughter of the house, a Señorita Consuela Deveruex y Lopez, as she signed the checks. There was nothing saying why Devil Dave's big sister had been left in charge. But that wasn't too tough to figure. What was tougher to figure was why Devil Dave had taken to holding up banks instead of just acting crazy mean. Maybe there'd be something explaining that in those land office files he'd asked old Henry to rustle up before he went home.

Longarm glanced up hopefully when the door swung open. Then he saw it wasn't old Henry standing there with two arms full of dusty ledgers.

It was that aptly nicknamed Miss Bubbles from the stenographers pool. They called her Miss Bubbles because everything about her seemed to be as globular as anything could get while it managed to stay pretty. So a big round bun of blonde hair perched atop her pretty oval face, from which big round eyes stared innocent as hell, considering how innocent Miss Bubbles was when another body got to know her. Longarm stared up uncertainly at the globular breasts staring back at him from atop the books she was toting as he quietly said, "Evening, Miss Bubbles. I was expecting old Henry, and how come you don't have anything on but them shoes and socks at the moment?"

The blonde shut the door behind her with a playful bump from her globular bare behind as she calmly replied, "Henry had a supper date with another chum. So I told him I'd take good care of you and you know full well I'm a woman of my word, Custis!"

Longarm gulped and said, "I sure do, and I told you how much I enjoyed it, Miss Bubbles. But I thought we agreed it wasn't too wise to mix our private lives with our jobs, here in the same building."

She dropped the pile of books he'd asked for on the desk in front of him to stand there bold as brass and naked as a jay in the flattering lamplight, hands on globular bare hips, as she pouted, "You were planning the ruination of poor Elsbeth, weren't you? What did she have to offer that I haven't already given you, you brute?"

It wasn't easy, but Longarm kept a straight face as he assured her and the other ladies from the stenographers pool that he'd never even spoken to the poor gal murdered that very day.

Miss Bubbles shrugged her rounded bare shoulders and replied, "You were getting ready to. She told us so, herself."

Longarm felt no call to fight the sheepish smile that crossed his face as he confessed, "That's the trouble with messing with the gals where you work. Like I told you, it always gets around the whole blamed building and you never know who's likely to take it the wrong way."

Miss Bubbles moved closer to perch her bare rump on a corner of the desk as she assured him, "I wasn't jealous of poor Elsbeth. I knew she was cherry. She told us so herself, poor thing. So I knew that once you'd tried in vain you'd

21

come limping back to this more willing blonde with your poor throbbing organ grinder.''

She ground her bare crotch around on the corner of the desk to ask in a huskier tone just how hard he might be at the moment.

Longarm laughed and insisted, ''I never stayed after hours to worry about such matters, no offense. I didn't even know you were still in the building and I really have to go through those federal ratifications of old Spanish land grants!''

To which she demurely replied, ''I did stay in the building when Henry told me you'd be in here working late. So we're all alone up here and you've got all night to paw through those fool books after you've pawed me some and screwed me a lot to make up for even considering another woman when you had all this waiting for you, ready and willing!''

Longarm started to argue. But life was too short to spend more than a man had to, arguing with women. So, thinking back to what a friendly whorehouse madam had told her working girls about just getting down and dirty to get it over with, he rose to toss his hat aside and haul Miss Bubbles in for a stand-up kiss.

She kissed back like an eager pup with a dirty mind and then laughed up at him because she said his tobacco tweed pants tickled her bare flesh.

He told her it was what she got for shaving her twat. She pouted that if he really wanted to please her he'd shave off his own pubic hair so's they could fornicate like innocent babes. That was what Miss Bubbles called a chubby grown woman with no hair on her snatch, an innocent babe. But he had to admit it felt inspiring down yonder as he took the matter in hand, but warned, ''Not in here. Have you forgot how silly you felt, hiding bareass under this same desk that time the judge came back to these chambers after hours?''

She finished unbuttoning his fly and hauled out his dawning erection to lead him by it as she assured him she knew just the place.

He let her haul him by his throbbing virility through the

22

anteroom and out in the dark marble corridor, even though he protested, "Damn it, honey, they do have a night watchman on duty!"

She assured him she knew what she was doing. He had to allow that she seemed to when they made it into another office suite without getting caught in the corridor as their heels echoed on bare marble.

Miss Bubbles was one of those lusty amourists who liked to fornicate by lamplight in front of a mirror whenever she had the chance. So Longarm suspected she'd put some thought into the love nest she'd thrown together in a side room of what she said was a vacant office a disbanded government agency had moved their stuff out of. Miss Bubbles had moved a padded leather sofa, a lamp table, and a swamping pier glass in to reflect on anything she might want to try with anyone aboard that sofa and her globular charms. So Longarm sat beside her on the smooth black leather and watched himself take off his own duds. It hardly seemed fair. But, unlike a frisky gal, a man had to haul his boots off before he could get out of his pants.

So the literally bubbly blonde was squirming her bare ass on smooth leather like a cat in heat by the time Longarm had his sixgun on the lamp table and himself on one knee to suit her pleasure. She rolled on her elbows and knees to thrust her double-bubble derriere up at him for a down-home dog-style entrance.

Longarm was just as glad. It wouldn't have been fair to call a gal who did it for free a whore. But when a gal made herself as available as Miss Bubbles it felt sort of silly to kiss her sincere.

As he entered her lush wet warmth from behind and she arched her spine for more, he reflected on how she might feel much the same about romantic mush. But however she might feel about what he was doing to her, she sure gave one hell of a ride.

"What are you grinning about?" she suddenly demanded, as Longarm realized she was watching them going at it dog-style. So he confided, "I ain't grinning at your pretty ass, Miss Bubbles. I was just reminded of this dumb joke I heard."

Before she bit down on his thrusting manhood she said, "We do look sort of silly in the mirror, considering how sweet it feels. What was the joke?"

He said, "I ain't sure how it applies to us. I don't see why it just came back to me. But it seems this old Papist priest was riding in a railroad club car with this rabbi of the Hebrew persuasion, the both of 'em sipping cider as fellow travelers will until they finally got around to confessing sins they'd have never told anybody they knew about."

Miss Bubbles moaned, "Ooh, faster! Harder! I promise not to tell if you make me come this beastly way! What had those other dirty old men have to confess in that joke? I don't find it funny, so far."

Longarm got a good grip on either hip bone to satisfy her flesh as he tried to satisfy her curiosity with, "This old rabbi swore the old priest to secrecy and confessed he'd ate a ham sandwich one time, just to see what all the fuss was about. So the priest said eating ham was just a kid sin next to what he'd done, just one time. The rabbi had to order another round to get it out of him, but he finally got the priest to admit he'd done this to a woman once."

Miss Bubbles moaned, "I'm so happy for him. But what's the point of the silly joke? Isn't a joke supposed to be funny?"

Longarm said, "I hadn't finished. The joke ends with the rabbi sadly deciding that if a man aims to sin his way to hell, a woman has a ham sandwich beat by a mile. So Powder River and let her buck!"

So the two of them came and somehow wound up on the floor face-to-face and still coming as they swapped spit and swore they'd never part again no matter what.

Then Miss Bubbles sprang up to reach for the duds she'd hung on a wall hook, patting her hair bun back in shape with the other hand while Longarm stared up from the floor on one elbow, sort of bemused.

She asked, "Do you really need all those land-grant ratifications, darling?"

He said, "West Texas grants for sure. There was nothing in the other records to indicate other family holdings in other parts. Young Devil Dave seems to run home to that same Lopez Grant every time he gets in real trouble anywhere else."

She said she'd be right back. He rose to his hands and knees to fish some matches and a three-for-a-nickel cheroot from the crumpled duds on the floor with him. He got back on the sofa to light up, with the smooth leather making his bare ass feel sort of wicked as he considered women and their mysterious ways. He'd been wondering how to gracefully get out of all this slap-and-tickle with the office punch board. So it was sort of surprising to feel relieved she'd be coming right back. The unfair sex was forever springing such surprises on mere men. That was likely why men spent so much time considering their mysterious ways.

As he sat there blowing smoke rings Longarm idly wondered whether Miss Bubbles shared his mingled feelings of delight and distaste for such late-night slap-and-tickle atop office furniture meant for more officious government business. He'd meant what he said when he'd told the unpredictable blonde they were asking for trouble, and Miss Bubbles had sounded sincere when she'd agreed they ought to quit whilst they were ahead. Almost getting caught, more than once, had convinced them both, or Longarm, at any rate, that the pleasures of carefree rutting with a casual acquaintance weren't worth the risk to a good government job. But it sure beat-all how tough it was to leave that last chocolate in the box, that last peanut in a bowl on the Parthenon bar, or pass on a sure piece of ass where you worked.

So he couldn't help from grinning like a shit-eating dog when Miss Bubbles nipped back in with just one of the bound ledgers from Judge Dickerson's desk across the way. She dropped it on the tufted leather by his bare hip and commenced to get undressed some more as Longarm reached for the heavy tome with his cheroot still gripped between his teeth, saying, "Hold the thought whilst I just look one or two things up, honey. You'll find I screw better with an easy mind. All the time we were at it, the last time, part of my brain was in West Texas instead of up your sweet little ring-dang-doo!"

She hung her spring frock back on the same hook and strode back to rejoin him in just her black lisle stockings and high button shoes as she told him to read all he wanted about West Texas land grants.

So he began to as Miss Bubbles sank gracefully to the floor with a bare elbow on the sofa and her hand on his bare thigh.

The rebel state of Texas had yet to win back the rights they'd once had to store such information in their Austin statehouse. It had been the United States who'd signed the Treaty of Guadalupe Hidalgo with Mexico to end their war back in '48. One of the terms agreed to was that the federal government would guarantee old Spanish land grants recognized by Mexico in earlier treaties, no matter what the new states and territories of California, Texas, and the New Mexico, since divided into Arizona and New Mexico Territories, might want.

Opening the tome to a map of West Texas, Longarm mused out loud how the Deveruex-Lopez Grant had to be somewhere close to where those three Texas counties met. He added, "I'd have heard tell of it if it was half as big as that million and three-quarters Beaubien-Miranda Grant that old Don Lucien Maxwell bought off the last Beaubien heirs further north along the Pecos. But it can't be too small. You ain't allowed to divide one of them land grants up. All bets are off as soon as you commence carving up the original gift from the king of Spain and, no offense, Miss Bubbles, but I'm trying to read these old records!"

Miss Bubbles didn't answer. Miss Bubbles couldn't answer, with her mouth so full.

Chapter 4

Miss Bubbles had to be home alone by eleven lest her neighbors suspect her of less than she'd been up to. Longarm offered her hack fare but she seemed to feel that might call her amateur status into question. So in the end he wound up in his own hired digs on the less fashionable side of Cherry Creek before midnight with his notebook filled with the little anyone knew for certain about Devil Dave and his home range along the lower Pecos.

The odds were fair that Deveruex and his pals would steer clear of the Deveruex-Lopez Grant long enough to make certain nobody was hot on their trail. So Longarm headed for West Texas the next morning, armed with a blanket, a federal warrant, and a tall story to go with his simple but time-tested disguise.

Outlaw eyes grew keen along the owlhoot trail, and nobody but stage actors at some distance from the front row could hope to fool anybody who was really looking with fake beards or putty noses. But, thanks to the pestiferous dress code of the Hayes Reform Administration, Longarm had been sitting in court near the late Elsbeth Flagg clean shaven, save for his permitted mustache, in that three-piece tobacco tweed suit and shoestring tie, with his dark telescoped Stetson mostly on that table, and the tailored grips of his cross-drawn

Colt '78 hidden from the view of anybody casing the court-room ahead of that fusillade.

A gunfighter accustomed to a double-action sixgun and a Winchester '73 loading the same .44–40 S&W rounds had no call packing any other brands of sidearm or saddle gun, and the double derringer Longarm had clipped to one end of his watch chain was nobody's business but his own.

He aimed to keep wearing his sixgun cross-draw. The lower slung buscadero side-draw favored by some quick-draw artists really did offer a split second edge in a face-to-face showdown, standing tall. After that, a sixgun in a side-draw holster was much more awkward to get at sitting down or on horseback, if it didn't fall out of the holster whilst you mounted up in a hurry. So Longarm stuck with the safer and surer style of gun toting proven in action by the likes of Hickok and the less famous but way deadlier young new-comer from Tennessee, Commodore Perry Owens. Longarm settled for a used but fancy tooled leather cross-draw rig he picked up in a hock shop along Larimer Street. He already had a faded denim outfit, and the notion of wearing some broke stranger's boots had little appeal to him. But a pair of pawned spurs, fancied up Border Style with coin-silver, inlaid against a gunmetal-blue ground, made his broken-in and un-polished army stovepipes seem more cow. Meanwhile a man could get around faster on foot with low heels, and Longarm was so tall that he didn't seem to be walking lower than most riders.

On most field missions Longarm brought his personal army saddle and bridle along, with his Winchester and possibles lashed to the same. But General McClellan hadn't included a roping horn when he'd designed that popular cavalry seat. So Longarm had his Winchester and usual saddle bags lashed to the double-rig and tie-down stock-saddle riding on the bag-gage rack in the private Pullman compartment he'd hired for the long round-about train ride to West Texas.

He hadn't asked to ride so fancy. Marshal Billy Vail had ordered it. The duck-soup simple plan his boss had reluctantly gone along with hinged on nobody suspecting Longarm's assumed name and occupation. A stranger drifting in from the west as a cow hand thrown out of work in the wake of the recent Lincoln County War was likely to have some awkward questions to answer if somebody else remembered riding a train down from Denver with the suspicious cuss.

So he stayed in his compartment and had his meals delivered at some extra cost, cussing Billy Vail and his own luck whenever he spied a well-turned ankle getting on at more than one stop. But all things good and bad must end, and he got off at last in El Paso to hole up at once in a posada he knew there run by friendly Mexicans.

He knew gals in El Paso of all complexions and persuasions. But the kindly old philosopher who'd warned a woman's tongue could wag more than a dog's tail had likely passed through parts where he was bettter known as a lawman than as an unemployed cowboy. So he holed up overnight in the posada to break any sign he'd left leaving the railroad depot and hired a Mex barkeep he trusted to buy him a good Spanish riding mule and tether it out back.

Then he rode off down the Rio Grande by the dawn's early light with a hard-on for that pretty little thing who'd served him *huevos ranchero* with his black coffee, in bed. He'd suspected she'd been anxious to serve him in other ways, but whether she'd have bragged or not, she'd been a daughter of the house and Longarm got along better than most of his own kind with Spanish-speaking folk because he played by their rules when it came to *mujares*. There were *mujares*, or women, along the border anybody could mess with and there were others nobody messed with, unless he was up to licking all their male kin, out to kissing cousins. You never even mentioned any gal in a Mex pal's family before you'd been introduced to her, formal, if you wanted said Mex to stay a pal. So whilst it was safe to thank a pretty little *mestiza* for a swell breakfast she'd been told to bring you, nothing any woman could possibly do for any man would be worth the risk of trying for it under her dad's own roof.

The first thing riders noticed about West Texas was the size of the place. Even when you beelined, it was over three hundred and fifty miles, or nigh two weeks in the saddle from El Paso, to where the Pecos drained into the Rio Grande, or Rio Bravo as most Mexicans still called her.

Back in Denver, Longarm and Billy Vail had agreed this might be good or bad. Unless Devil Dave and his pals already had a lead on him, Longarm figured to dawdle in ahead of them but not too soon after word of their gunplay got spread across their home range. With Longarm's wary agreement, Billy Vail had wired Texas Ranger Headquarters in San Antone about that federal warrant on their wandering boy. San Antone was a tad closer to the the Pecos Valley than El Paso and naturally, there were ranger substations even closer. So unless the rangers got luckier than usual, they should have paid their usual calls on the usual suspects and suspected hiding places by the time Longarm could ride in from another direction entire. In the unlikely event the rangers caught Devil Dave by the time he arrived—they'd had a wet spring and the water holes one called tanks in West Texas were full and the grass grew green amid the mesquite, prickle pear, and Spanish bayonet—so, what the hell, a nice long ride for nothing wouldn't leave any permanent scars and a man got rusty around that infernal federal building.

He'd picked a saddle mule for the first day on the trail with some distance in mind. You could get thirty miles a day out of a cavalry mount without hurting it. A Spanish saddle mule would carry you ten miles further, easy, in such balmy spring weather. So Longarm tried for that and rode in around sundown to the dinky settlement around a Butterfield stage stop in the severely eroded Finlay Mountains. Then he paid for extra care for his somewhat lathered mule and checked into a posada early and alone after a snack by dusk at an open-to-the-street tamale stand. He neither tried to get noticed nor shouted for attention before he turned in early with some magazines and plenty of smokes.

In the morning he rose early and swapped the mule and a

few dollars more for a paint cowpony who'd seen better days. Her main attraction for a lawman on an undercover mission was her local brand.

He rode her hard, albeit less hard than he had the bigger mule, and made it to a bigger trail town where the mountains flattened out some and he got to ride through cattle range a spell. The complicated tangle of modestly high but rugged ranges to the west of the Stockton Plateau were dubbed the Davis Mountains on most maps and cropped up some more south of the Rio Grande as Old Mexico's Burro Mountains. Longarm drove the paint mare as far as Allamoore, a handy stop in the low pass through the main Davis range on a harder uphill push the next day and, this time, let it be loudly known he was sick and tired of a muley old mare off the Rocking H, who'd gone lame on him goddamn her eyes.

So there were other Texicans and Mexicans listening with interest by the municipal corral as the stranger who allowed they could call him anything but "Late For Breakfast" dickered with an old Mex horse trader for a fresher mount, come morning.

They'd about settled on the paint and a few dollars more when an older Anglo sporting a brass star on his vest drifted across from the town lock-up, taking in Longarm's faded denims and tailored gun grips as he came, casually placing his gun hand on the butt of his Navy Colt Conversion before he quietly asked, "Might you have a bill of sale for that pony from the Rocking H remuda, cowboy?"

Longarm had one, but that was no way to get famous in Texas. So he puffed up a tad and demanded, "Are you calling me a horse thief, little darling?"

The town law soberly replied, "I ain't nobody's darling. I'm the town marshal and a deputy sheriff of Hudspeth County combined. So would you care to show me a bill of sale for that mare, come along to the telegraph office with me, or fill your damn fist? It don't make no nevermind to me at my age. I got to this age by beating fresh young squirts to the draw."

31

Some of the onloookers standing close crawfished back from what was starting to shape up as impending doom. Longarm let the tension build enough to ensure some gossip. Then he smiled sheepishly at the gruff old lawman and said, "Don't get your bowels in an uproar, Mr. Law. I'll show you the infernal bill of sale if it means that much to you, for Pete's sake."

The older lawman tensed even more as Longarm reached inside his denim bolero jacket for the simple bill of sale he'd asked for when he'd tossed in those extra dollars with that mule. Being county law, the old timer knew the names of most county residents authorized to trade in horseflesh on a regular basis. So when Longarm handed the terse contract over, he read it fast, nodded curtly, and handed it back as he growled, "Why didn't you just produce your damned bill of sale as soon as I asked for it? What sort of a name is Crawford, and are we supposed to be afraid of you because you pack a double-action?"

Longarm shook his head and said, "I've been told Crawford is a Scotch name. You'd have to ask the uncle they named me after what a Duncan might be."

The local lawman decided, "That's a Scotch name as well, sometimes. Now tell us what you're doing here in Allamoore, Mr. Duncan Crawford."

Longarm answered simply. "Trying to get me a better mount. Couldn't you tell? This greaser and me were about to spit and shake on yonder roan when you horned in just now."

The portly Mexican asked who he was calling a greaser.

Longarm laughed lightly and said, "I apologize, Amigo. I didn't know you were Irish. Do you want to sell that fucking roan or don't you?"

The town law quietly observed there was no call to talk nasty to good old Gordo.

Longarm shrugged and said, "I never invited any of 'em into Texas. I had kin at the Alamo and I'm pleased as punch about my daddy's ride through Old Mexico in '47. Might you have a horse-trade in mind your ownself or can I work something out with this greaser about yonder roan?''

They were still fussing about his manners as a rat-faced kid in white cotton, a serape, and a straw sombrero scuttled across the way to join an older Mexican seated at a sidewalk table in a silver mounted *charro* outfit, sipping *cerveza*.

As the sneak joined him, staying on his feet with sombrero in hand, the prosperous looking rider quietly asked, "*¿Que piensete?*"

The kid he'd sent closer to listen in replied, "*¡Pienso que no, me patron!* The tall build is right. The Colorado crush of his sombrero is right. The double-action Colt carried crossdraw is right. *Pero el hombre* called Longarm by *los Yanguis* and *El Brazo Largo* by those of our *raza* is said to be *muy simpatico*. That big gringo across the *calle* is a *pendejo chingado* begging for a fight with old Gordo!''

The dapper rider he'd reported this too shrugged and decided, "Is Gordo's problem. Is just as well for *us* he is only another gringo with an ugly mouth. Perhaps he won that hat from some Colorado rider, if he did not steal it. Let those he insults directly worry about him.''

The younger and shabbier Mexican nodded and shot the tall tanned stranger across the way a thoughtful look as he decided, "He is a big one and that Colt has tailored grips. For why did you think he might be the famous *El Brazo Largo, me patron*?''

His boss sipped some more iced beer before he replied in a casual tone he didn't really feel, "Some others I do business with from time to time asked us to keep an eye out for such a famous hunter of men.''

"They worry that *El Brazo Largo* could be hunting for one of them?'' asked the sneak who'd dismissed Longarm as a drifting bully boy.

The hired gun asked to stop Longarm at all costs from getting anywhere near the Pecos shrugged and replied, "*¿Quien sabe?* Perhaps it is one of them. Perhaps it is only someone they know. What can I tell you? I only work here. If he gets past us he is *their* problem.''

33

Chapter 5

And so it went for the better part of a fortnight, riding rough country, building a rep for the hitherto unheard-of Dunk Crawford. He got invited in for cake, coffee, and gossip at most homespreads you'd pass where the nearest neighbors lived miles away and nobody delivered any morning papers. As a rule Longarm was as likely to stop and visit with Mexicans, Indians, or any other friendly folk. But knowing he was known as *El Brazo Largo* along the border by both decent Mexicans and the Diaz Dictatorship's ferocious *Federales y Rurales*, he decided it would be safer and better for his image if he avoided any dealings with Spanish-speaking folk that close to the border. In West Texas that included most Indians—peaceful Caddo as well as Mission-Apache of not-so-certain disposition. Full Quill Bronco Apache raiding along both sides of the border under Victorio at the moment spoke uncertain Spanish and just enough English to say, "Die, mother fucker!" So it didn't seem likely he'd have to worry about fooling that bunch about his real name. With any luck the 10th Cav had Victorio on the run in Old Mexico in any case. The Buffalo Soldiers of the Colored 10th Cav made Indians nervous. This was partly because the army had been able to pick and choose between ex-slaves anxious to soldier and party because the resulting well-trained troopers were tough for some Indians to classify. The Lakota defined a man of color as a *wasichusapa*, which could be translated literally as black whiteman. NaDéné, or so-called Apache, got around the confusion by just avoiding the 10th Cav as much as they could manage. Things Indians had trouble describing to a "tee" were inclined to be viewed as bad medicine.

In the trail town of Toyah along the San Martine Draw, he got into an ugly facedown in the Cottonwood Saloon that never went past the two of them stepping away from the bar as everyone else gave them a whole lot of room. For it seldom did, and, whilst Cockeyed Jack McCall had overdone such bullshit by shooting Hickok all the way, most hard hairpins built their reps on almost-fights.

John Wesley Hardin and Hickok himself had gained stature at no cost to either just by glowering at one another that time in Abilene. So Longarm could hope his brush with destiny in the form of the mean town drunk of Toyah might convince others he was an armed and dangerous asshole. A true specimen of the breed would have slapped leather on a man too nasty natured to abide and too drunk to beat a schoolmarm to the draw as he stood there cussing and drooling.

By that time more than one pest had commented on the telescoped Colorado or North Range crush of Longarm's coffee-brown Stetson. He'd considered another hat before he'd left Denver, wearing the one molded to his skull by some time and toil.

A new hat always looked new until you'd worn it some, whether you stomped on it, pissed on it, or let a pony drink out of it more than once. His broken-in Stetson's dark felt crown would look like it had been telescoped a spell and then reshaped if he punched its crown into the more common Texas peak with a crease down the front, and he didn't want to be taken for even an ex–Texas Ranger. So he told those who asked polite what he'd said earlier about being out of work in the wake of the Lincoln County War. That range was still new enough for riders from all over to be riding it in all sorts of outfits, and, since he didn't care to go on about things

36

he only knew from heresay, his terse, if not evasive, answers about up New Mexico way (New Mexico being north of the western reaches of West Texas), seemed to convince West Texans more that Dunk Crawford was bad news leftover from the mutually suicidal shootout between the Murphy-Dolan and Chisum-McSween factions. When asked which side he might have ridden for, "Crawford" growled he disremembered, in a tone that discouraged further questions along those lines.

When asked if he knew Billy The Kid he just smiled through gents as he allowed he knew The Kid by rep and might have met him now and again.

This was the pure truth as soon as you studied on it. For had a U.S. Deputy Marshal been dead certain that shyly smiling youth who'd bought him that beer had been a wanted outlaw, he'd have never been able to give him that break.

When asked what he thought of that new territorial governor who'd cleaned up New Mexico, Longarm, as Crawford, dryly said he'd read some of that book about Ben Hur that Governor Lew Wallace had written.

It seemed safe to opine that Major Murphy had died broke of booze and pneumonia or that his pal, Jim Dolan, had been ruined by the feud as well. Everyone knew Tunstall and McSween on the other side had been killed along with their top gun, Dick Brewer, leaving his young henchman, The Kid, on the run whilst Uncle John Chisum had holed up on his South Spring ranch, feeling old and scared shitless by the trouble he and his own pals had stirred up to begin with, if the truth would be known. Nobody on either side had shown a lick of sense or made a dime extra out of the Lincoln County War. So Longarm's excuses for looking for work to the Southeast made sense, while the surly attitude he'd assumed had more than one West Texan almost certain he'd lost a job that had called for tailored grips on his Colt '78, loading .44-40.

That same stage magician's shemale assistant had taught him about letting the audience outsmart its fool self that way.

She'd explained one night in bed how surprised folk were when they thought they had a trick figured out and the magician produced a different result. She'd said you could get them to picture all sorts of trapdoors and mirrors that weren't where they thought by not stopping them from thinking you'd gone to more trouble than you had. As a peace officer he'd already noticed how bullshit artists tended to give themselves away by telling you more than you'd ever asked them. Few had any call to doubt a man who simply said he'd ridden in the war. It was when he got into all the charges he'd led into the cannon's mouth that got folk to wondering. Longarm knew that nobody would have believed him for a minute if he'd claimed he'd been the one who'd shot either Rancher Tunstall or Sheriff Brady. But as long as he only allowed he'd been close enough to the costly mess for it to have cost him, nobody had any call to doubt him. It was less important what they thought he might have been up to in New Mexico Territory a spell back than it might have been to explain why he'd come down from Colorado, more recent.

The scattered spurs of the Davis Mountains flattened out to turn into the Stockton Plateau. The lower Pecos Valley lay between that and the Edwards Plateau to the east, with the former Comanche home range on the Staked Plains more to the northeast. By this time, of course, not many Indians, quill or tame, haunted their former hunting grounds on marginal range, which was being rapidly covered with livestock and mesquite. The earlier buffalo herds had been hell on mesquite and other chaparral.

He got into another tense discussion over a friendly game of Five Card Stud and then he was down in the valley of the Pecos, somewhat north of that Deveruex-Lopez Grant, south of Sheffield-Crossing.

He timed his arrival in Sheffield-Crossing on a dusty cordovan gelding for just after noon, hoping the few dusty streets would be cleared for La Siesta, which was followed by sensible Anglos, as well as Mexicans in West Texas, for the same reasons of health.

Neither Mexicans nor Southerners who hid indoors from the worst heat of day—days could get seriously hot—were lazy, as some outsiders thought. But even in Ante Bellum Dixie, where the Planter Folk had led more sporting lives, they'd gotten in most of their social gatherings and fox hunting during the early morn or evening hours. All the flirty belles knocked off around noon to undress and doze fitfully upstairs during the hotter hours, only to come back down gussied up in their hoop skirts for dancing and fan-fluttering that could go on past midnight, when all industrious New Englanders were fast asleep.

Longarm thought he'd timed things right as he passed the first houses on the outskirts of town. There wasn't much stirring when he rode down the one main street toward the river and reined in out front of the one livery stable. He rustled up a dozed-off Caddo kid to care for his damned pony. As the Indian watered and fed the gelding in its hired stall (You never fed a pony *before* you watered it.), Longarm stored his roping saddle in their tack room, but hung on to his Winchester and draped the center strap of his two saddlebags over his left arm. Anyone desperate enough to steal his old bedroll was welcome to the summerweight flannel blankets, canvas tarp, or rolled-in slicker and chaps.

He tipped the young Caddo a dime extra and asked about any hotel or posada they might have in Sheffield-Crossing. The Indian kid said he just worked there at the livery. They didn't serve Indians anywheres else in town. Sheffield-Crossing was a cow town of recent vintage. So most everyone who had anything to say there was an unreconstructed reb.

Longarm stepped out into the now dazzling sunlight with his rifle cradled over his saddlebags, the grips of his sixgun peeking out from under them, with his gun hand free.

He was mildy surprised but felt no great concern when he saw a baker's dozen of dismounted riders lined up on the shady side of the street in front of an inviting-looking saloon.

39

That reminded Longarm he hadn't had anything stronger than homespread coffee all day. So he started across the wide, dusty street to do something about that. But one of the riders on the far side, in a pair of pony-hide chaps with a matching vest, bellowed out, "Stay put, you rude bastard! Show some respect for the damned dead!"

Longarm was fixing to stride on over and ask the cuss who's death he had in mind when he heard the drums of the dead march and glanced up the street to the west to see . . . nothing at all.

But somebody had to be beating that mournsome drum. So Longarm stayed put and, sure enough, a raggedy uniformed band with just the one drummer drumming a snare covered with black muslin, came out of a side street to swing their way, followed shortly by a rubber-tired hearse drawn by a handsome black team with plumed harness. As it drew nearer you could see the silver-handled mahogany coffin through the plate glass sides of the hearse. Whoever they were fixing to plant had died rich, it was safe to assume. A full platoon of mourners were following afoot, with one Mex kid gussied up in a silver-trimmed black *charro* outfit, leading a freshly groomed palomino, saddled *vaquero* style with polished wood showing, where Anglo saddle trees were leather covered. The saddle was empty. Two tall, tooled *vaquero* boots rode backwards in the stirrups with their big spur rowels leading.

The mourners seemed a mixed bag of Anglo, Mex, and in-between, all wearing their Sunday best, which seemed to make folk look more like their ancestors than the everyday work duds worn by everybody did.

One gal in particular caught Longarm's eye. She strode down the street as if she owned it, despite her respectful expression as she followed the dead man's mount. She was dressed for riding, herself, in a black Spanish habit and one of those flat-topped black hats with fly tassels dangling all around the edge of the broad brim. Her complexion was that odd orange shade you never saw on any man or any woman who didn't descend from whatever part of Old Spain such an unusual peachy hide called for. As she disdainfully glanced his way, he saw her big old eyes flash hazel. Her hair was swept up under a hat the color of old gold braid. She sure was something and he couldn't blame her for dismissing him as some saddle tramp. He'd been busting a gut trying to be taken for a saddle tramp.

As the hearse passed, most of the riders in front of the saloon on the far side made the sign of the cross. For all the mean things they said about Mexicans, or perhaps because of them, a heap of so-called Texas Anglos were Irish Catholics. Spain and then Mexico had encouraged swarms of such folk from the British Isles to settle their province of Texas in the vain hope they'd form an English-speaking Catholic buffer between Old Mexico and the alarming Yanqui Heretics.

Longarm had spent enough time around Papists on both sides of the border to know how it was done. But he had no call to lie about religion to a dead man he'd never met, so far as he knew, and simply removed his hat to show some respect as, just before the passing hearse blocked his view across the street, he spotted something that didn't seem quite right.

He wasn't sure what he'd seen. It was one of those odd shifts in the regular scenery of life that you sometimes catch out the corner of one eye. By the time the rear of the hearse passed on to expose them all again, they'd finished . . . what had they been doing all at the same time?

They'd been making the sign of the cross. All the same way. Or had one of them done it backwards? As if he'd been faking it, without too much Catholic Sunday School under his belt.

By the time the whole procession had passed and Longarm saw they were heading toward the crossing the town was named for, as if they meant to bury the poor cuss on the far side, he'd decided it hardly mattered whether one of those cow hands had just tried to show the same respect as his real Papist pals or whether he'd been brought up in another faith that did things different. Nobody back home in West-By-God,

Virginia, had crossed themselves any which way. But he'd heard or read there were furriners who called themselves Catholics but couldn't seem to agree what day Easter might fall on. Praying too much could get a body in as much trouble as never praying at all.

Longarm glanced heavenward and muttered, "I'm fixing to have a nice cool pitcher of suds now, Lord. Feel free to send me a sign if you don't want me to."

He strode through the crowd out front to beat them all inside. He dropped his saddlebags and Winchester on a corner table and moved to the bar to pay for a pitcher of draft beer and two tumblers. Then he set up in that corner with his possibles on the floor and the rifle across his lap to see if anybody aimed to join him. For getting a town drunk talking in a small town was as easy a way to horn in as going to their barber when you didn't really need a haircut.

His eyes were just getting used to the dimmer light of the saloon when he spied someone drifting over, outlined by the sunlight through the swinging doors beyond.

Then an all too familiar figure sat down, wearing the circled five-pointed star of the Texas Rangers on his trail-dusted white shirt as he said, "Afternoon, Longarm. What brings you to Sheffield-Crossing, that bust-out up Denver way?"

Longarm rolled his eyes up at the pressed-tin ceiling as he sighed and muttered, "Oh, Lord, you might have sent me this sign before I paid for all this beer!"

Chapter 6

Hoping against hope it wasn't too late, Longarm murmured, "The name is Crawford, Duncan Crawford, off the Diamond K in New Mexico Territory if you follow my meaning, Ranger Travis."

The ranger replied no louder, "I follow your drift, even though I thought the Diamond K was in Colorado and that reporter for the Denver Post signed his newspaper stories Crawford. I remember them from when I was up that way to deliver a federal warrant. They were about this good old boy who took me over to that Parthenon Saloon. Speaking of which, is this my glass?"

Longarm poured the tumbler closest to the ranger as he tried as hard as he could not to look up and see if anyone else was close enough to worry about. Glancing around, like a kid fixing to shoplift a stick of candy, was a certain way to look worried.

But none of the booted feet he could take in without looking up seemed to be standing within easy earshot. So Longarm risked quietly observing, "I've heard there was another Diamond K outside of Denver. I doubt anybody in these parts would have much to say to that reporter or the lawman he writes all those tall stories about."

Ranger Travis sipped some suds and allowed he knew the

feeling as Longarm filled his own tumbler. As Longarm drank, the ranger quietly told him, "I was just fixing to pack it in after riding high, low, and sideways in these parts after an escaped federal prisoner. For some reason nobody he grew up with remembers him at all. He ain't down the valley at his home spread on the Deveruex-Lopez Grant. He ain't at any of many a line shack they have spread out across all that property, and he ain't at the townhouse the Widow Deveruex has here in Sheffield-Crossing. Ain't that a bitch?"

Longarm cautiously replied, "I'd be sort of suprised to find a known killer at his officious home address when the law came calling. As for his local kith and kin, nobody ever gets along with everybody in his family, and they don't call him Devil Dave because he's unusually easy to get along with. You mark my words and see if somebody they trust won't betray Frank and Jesse, now that there's bounty money posted on 'em."

Ranger Travis asked, "Why are we talking about the James Boys? I thought we were after Devil Dave Deveruex, ah, Mr. Crawford."

Longarm explained, "Same deal. A wayward youth with more bullets than brains hiding out betwixt temper tantrums in a fair-sized neck of the chaparral, inhabited by a whole heap of locals the law can neither arrest nor get the right time of day from. You don't have to be a college professor to hold up a bank and run home to Momma. I know Devil Dave's old and ailing Mex mother spends most of her time in town these days. Tell me what you can about the daughter of the house who's said to be managing the family grant and business matters these days."

Ranger Travis sipped more suds and topped his tumbler by pouring without asking as he murmured, "You just saw her outside if that was you I was staring at from out front. I thought at first you were a lawman I knew from up Colorado way. Reckon it must have been that pork-pie hat."

Longarm said, "Nevermind my hat. The wind blows serious where I first learned the ropes of the beef industry. From

44

what we had on file I was given to understand the Deveruex-Lopez herd tallies over a thousand head and you say I just saw this shemale wonder?''

The ranger nodded to say, ''Miss Connie Deveruex. She leaves off the maternal Lopez and hates it when the greasers call her Doña Consuela. But she shares the proud Spanish notion that as soon as you can count your cows you own too few of 'em. She was walking behind that hearse just now. She sets a pony even prouder, sidesaddle.''

''Are we talking about a dusky blonde gal in black who stares at a man as if he was a bug on a pin?'' asked Longarm hopefully.

The ranger sighed and said, ''I wish she'd stared through me half that friendly when I called on her to ask about her baby brother. She invited me to supper and offered to put me up for the night. But that was only because she was Landed Irish on her daddy's side and Hidalgo Class on her momma's. Her eyes get innocent but her smile drips venom when you mention her kid brother. She swears she hasn't seen hide nor hair of him since he stopped the Butterfield Stage a good three years ago. She's lying, of course. Every time any of us cut the bastard's trail it leads us towards this valley before we lose it in the quicksands of '¿Quien Sabe?' That's what greasers say when they're too polite to tell you to go to hell. It means, Who Knows?''

Longarm muttered, ''I've noticed. I can manage a lick of Border Mex if I put my mind to it. I'd hesitate to tell any lawman where a kinsman or neighbor might be if I was still a farm boy back in West-By-God, Virginia. Such conversations can get you burned out if it don't get you or any of your kin murdered total. So there ain't no mystery about his kith and kin covering up for Devil Dave. What I don't understand entire is why they have to.''

He fished for a cheroot to nurse along with his beer as he went on. ''Most outright outlaws are in it because they really need the money. Clay Allison was a crazy-mean killer. King Fisher has to be touched in the head to run around in tiger-hide chaps picking fights, and Ben Thompson has killed men with guns, knives, or anything handy since he and his mean kid brother, Tom, arrived from Old England. But none of them mad dogs have ever robbed a bank because they simply had no call to!''

The ranger nodded and showboated a tad by observing, ''I follow your drift. The late Clay Allison supported his bad habits well enough with a spread and herd smaller than Connie Deveruex manages. King Fisher prefers ranching to robbing as a source of income, and, despite their disgusting ways, the Thompson brothers have usually gotten by as trail bosses or hired guns. What if Miss Connie just wouldn't give her kid brother an allowance? Many a minister's son has gone bad because his old man was tightwad, you know.''

Longarm shook his head and pointed out, ''The two of us just saw her alive and well out front. Would you expect a cold-blooded killer who's downed many an innocent bystander to hesitate sixty seconds if anybody at all was that mean to him?''

The ranger blurted, ''Hell, she's his own sister!'' before he thought through to, ''You're right. He could have arranged any number of tragic accidents and wound up the sole heir in the catbird seat if money and bossing honest riders around was enough to satisfy his twisted soul.''

Longarm nodded soberly and said, ''You missed the drawn-out trial he just put us through in Denver. He was guilty beyond the shadow of a flea in the dark. But he had this team of high-priced Texas lawyers raising objections to everything including the weather outside on the day his other pals shot up the courtroom and lit out with him. I can't see him having to rob because he's from a poor family. He robs because he just plain enjoys the scenery along the owlhoot trail!''

''When he ain't holed up on his home ground,'' the ranger grumbled.

Longarm shrugged and said, ''I never said any of 'em were college professors or even cowboys with common sense and natural habits. Who was Miss Connie showing respect to by following his hearse on foot? Some other local cattle baron?''

The ranger smiled thinly and replied, ''Not hardly. Just a greaser named Jesus. Jesus Robles. One of Miss Connie's *vaqueros*. He rode his pony into bob wire in the dark and busted his neck. They had to shoot the pony and some say old 'Soos was riding fast and drunk.''

Longarm lit the cheroot he'd stuck between his teeth before he shook out the waterproof waxed Mexican match to observe, ''There you go. A lady who'd treat a drunken cowboy to such a handsome funeral after he'd killed one of her mounts would hardly hold out on her own flesh and blood.''

Travis asked, ''What if he asked for more than she and her momma could afford? Speaking from sad family experience I can tell you a heap of big outfits live on credit and credit alone between market drives, with the beef prices set by fine-haired sons of bitches from back East!''

Longarm mentally studied the notes he'd taken in Denver and left there for safe keeping before he said, ''It works either way. Old Devil Dave's never pulled off a job that would have netted him more than a few hundred dollars after he'd split the swag with his sidekicks, and your point about cattlemen living on credit most of the time was well taken. I hear Uncle John Chisum lost a swamping amount from his bank account on that Lincoln County War. But the last time I had coffee and cake at his South Spring Ranch the coffee was Arbuckle Brand and the cake wasn't stale. Uncle John has this pretty little gal, Miss Sally, keeping house for him these days. He introduces her as his niece. She may well be his niece. My point is that Uncle John keeps her gussied up pretty and I suspect she charges all the coffee and cake she wants to on the credit anyone with a lot of land and beef on the hoof can command. I know Miss Connie Deveruex can't control as much land and beef on the hoof as Uncle John Chisum or Colonel Richard King, down where the Rio Grande flows into the Gulf. But her kid brother should have been able to charge

47

or borrow enough to get stewed, screwed, and tattooed enough to kill him.''

The ranger finished his tumbler and a half of suds and put his hand over the empty as he growled, ''I wish it had, and I got to get on down the owlhoot trail. Ah, Crawford, I'll tell my captain about this conversation. He'll likely go along with you riding solo to your doom. Lord knows we've had no luck and you have a rep for being lucky. But have you forgot what happened to them two Pinkerton men who rode into Clay County alone after Frank and Jesse that time?''

Longarm blew a thoughtful smoke ring and said, ''Nope. I've often wondered how they gave themselves away as undercover riders. The one who gunned the two of 'em has never seen fit to say.''

The ranger rose and held out a hand to part friendly. Longarm was too smart to glance around the crowded saloon as he quietly murmured he'd rather not shake.

Travis proved he could think on his own feet by raising his voice as he turned away, saying, ''Up your ass then you tight-lipped son of a clam!''

Longarm made a rude gesture at the ranger's back as Travis strode out in a huff.

Longarm poured himself some more suds but just sat there smoking until, sure enough, a rider who could have been Tex or Mex as he stood tall and tan in a gray *charro* outfit trimmed in black braid came over and sat down uninvited to place a Colt '73 Frontier on the table in front of him and say, ''I'd be Chongo Masters and I ride for the D Bar L. I feel somehow certain you're ready to answer some questions about now.''

Longarm drew his .44-40 with a left-handed twist-draw. He lifted the Winchester from his lap to slam them both on the table in front of himself as he calmly replied, ''I answer to Duncan Crawford these days. I don't ride for nobody and it depends on how polite your questions might be.''

It got mighty quiet in there for a serious breathless spell. Then Chongo Masters smiled thinly and said, ''I don't think

48

you savvy the situation here, Mister Crawford. I forgot to say most of these other boys ride for the D Bar L, too. They rode into town behind me, see?"

"You must be tired after dragging so many ponies after you," said Longarm, without taking his eyes off that one man and that one gun at the table with him as he added in a politer tone, "I never told you I wouldn't talk to you. I'm still waiting to hear your question, not a schoolyard-bully brag."

"Ay, que descarado!" marveled a Mex in the crowd.

An English-speaking rider growled, "Clean the sassy stranger's plow for him, Chongo."

Neither of them were staring into the sassy stranger's gun-muzzle gray eyes. Chongo managed to keep his own voice from cracking as he pasted a sickly smile across his swarthy face and confided, "You see how it is when there's no opera house in town and the ones making the most helpful suggestions ain't in the line of fire. Afore you cloud up and rain all over me, I only wanted to know what you and that ranger were talking about, just now."

Longarm asked, "How come? Might you be wanted by the Texas Rangers, Masters?"

The somewhat deflated local bully said, "Not hardly. I just told you I had a steady job, in charge of all the riding stock down on the Deveruex-Lopez spread. Me and the boys were only wondering whether that ranger was asking about anybody from around here that we might know."

Longarm had been thinking a lot harder than a poker player holding a straight flush and wondering who might be holding a royal. So his poker face gave nothing away as he shrugged and replied, "Like I told that nosy ranger, I got nothing to hide about anybody in these parts because I just drifted in from other parts. I'd have never made her as far as the Pecos if everywhere I stopped along the way they had coffee and cake for me but no job. I told that fool ranger I just rode in for the first time less than a full hour ago. So how in thunder was I supposed to tell him about some durned old Greek?"

Chongo blinked in confusion and studied some before he

said, "Hold on. Are you sure it was Greek Steve he was asking you about, not a Tex-Mex by the name of Dave?"

Longarm started to shake his head, brightened and replied, "Oh, sure, him too. Another cuss I never heard of, called Dave something or other. I told him I didn't know anybody called Greek Steve or Greek anything. Now I got a question. What's this shit about and how come they're pestering *me* about it?"

Chongo twisted in his seat to call out, "Hey, Pantages? Get over here and tell us what the rangers want you for!"

A burly rider with jet-black hair and a blue jaw but whiter skin than most of the bunch came over with a beer scuttle in hand, grabbing a chair from another table along the way.

As he swung it around to sit in like a pony, backwards, Chongo told him, "This is Duncan Crawford, Steve. He says that ranger he was just jawing with in here was asking questions about you."

Greek Steve stared hard at Longarm and flatly stated, "That is a fucking lie. I say this to your face, you lying bastard. So what are you going to do about it, eh?"

Chapter 7

Chongo had been staring into Longarm's eyes longer. So he was the the one who put a hand on the newcomer's sleeve to warn, "You're out of line, Greek Steve. It was that ranger who mentioned your name in vain, not Crawford, here."

Greek Steve said, "Bullshit! I ain't wanted by the fucking rangers for toad squat! I've been an upright and honest Pecos Valley boy since nine months after my momma came from Salmos as a bride to join my dear old dad in Texas! Anybody who says the Texas Rangers are after me is a lying bastard, like I said!"

Longarm flicked some ash from his cheroot and soberly observed it was just as well he hadn't lied, adding, "I'd have to kill you if it was me you were calling a bastard. Since I never said anybody was after you, it ain't too late to reason calm about what I might or might not have said about you to that ranger."

Chongo soothed, "There you go. Hear the man out, Greek Steve."

The belligerent Hellene didn't answer one way or the other. Longarm decided silence was at least gold-washed and said, "You're right that I had no call to say any lawman was after you, Mister Pantages. We can all agree that we never laid eyes on one another until mighty recent. I just now got here."

"From New Mexico, crowded out by the trouble they've been having up Lincoln County way," Chongo chimed in, adding, "he couldn't have been the one to bring your name up. He couldn't have known you were alive. Ain't that right, Crawford?"

Longarm nodded curtly and said, "That ranger never mentioned Mister Pantages by name. He only said he'd heard they had a Greek boy riding with the D Bar L and asked what I might know about him. I told him I had never been closer to any such outfit than I am right now and had no idea how many Greeks, Dutchmen, or Eskimos they might have riding for them. He intimated I was a liar, too. But he said it more polite and I never throw down on a lawman if I can possibly avoid it."

The two local riders exchanged puzzled glances. Greek Steve seemed more puzzled and less outraged as he demanded, "What did that fucking ranger accuse me of? I know he was accusing me because I'm the only Greek for miles. Texas Greek, that is. My folk talked Greek at home when I was a boy. I remember they called it *Elliniki*, but that's one of the few Greek words I still remember. My momma used to take me to the Greek Orthodox services whenever we got over to San Antone. But there ain't no Greek churches nor other Greek riders along the lower Pecos. So he must have meant me and what do you reckon that means?"

They both looked at Longarm. It wouldn't have been wise to mention that Greek Orthodox church up in Denver, where everybody standing on the steps crossed themselves different from Roman Catholics when they held their Easter Procession on a different day and tied up traffic all around. So he simply said, "You're asking the wrong man. I told that ranger he was asking the wrong man, too. He said he knew I was here to hire on at that D Bar L just down the valley. When I told him I'd done no such thing, that was when he called me a liar. He said he knew for a fact some lady was taking on extra help, and he called me a liar some more when I said that if I wanted to hire on as household help I'd have asked Miss

Sally Chisum for a job without having to leave New Mexico. She's the lady as keeps house at the Long-Rail and Jingle-Bob home spread at South Spring and . . .''

"Nevermind that range pirate and his famous play-pretty!" Chongo cut in, turning to Greek Steve to demand, "Are you sure you ain't got anything to tell Miss Connie about you-know-who? There ain't no way a stranger to these parts could make what this one's saying up out of thin air, even if he was a lawman, himself."

Longarm growled, "Aw, if you're going to keep insulting me, I'll thank you both to leave my damn table and let me drink in peace. I only fetched one extra glass from the bar in hopes they'd have some gals in this surly saloon. Since anyone can see it's just a piss-poor excuse for a dog-fighting pit, I'll just drink alone 'til it cools off enough to ride on."

Chongo said, "I wish you'd both cool off! That trouble-making tin star, combined with this noonday heat, has us all at loggerheads when we may be on the same side. It had to be that ranger asking all those questions about you and that trail-drive Miss Connie's been planning, Greek Steve. They must have you down as a schoolmate of you-know-who and they wouldn't know Miss Connie had us rounding up for that drive well before that . . . family emergency. I'd say the rangers have put one and one together to come up with seven or eleven!"

Greek Steve was staring at Longarm as he told Chongo, "I'd say you sure talk a lot in front of total-ass strangers, too. We don't know this saddle tramp from the Czar Of All The Russians and folk here in the valley don't talk about Miss Connie's personal problems amongst each other!"

Chongo started to argue, nodded, and told Longarm, "When he's right he's right. Greek Steve has a short fuse because he takes a little rawhiding about Greek Loving."

Greek Steve scowled and snapped, "Where I come from they say it's the Spanish who prefer ass fucking and the Irish who fuck their dear old mothers when they can't get the pigs to put out!"

53

Chongo sighed and said, "One of these days you're going to push me a tad too far, Greek Steve. But let's get cooled down some before we all blow up like cartridges in a frying pan."

He got back to his feet, adding, "I don't know about you sweating *buscaderos*, but I'm off to Rosalinda's for a cold shower and a naked flop on cool sheets until that fucking sun outside let's up for the day!"

Greek Steve allowed he could go for a *siesta* at Rosalinda's as well. So Longarm asked if they were talking about some nearby cooler posada.

The two local riders exchanged amused looks. Chongo said, "Come on along and judge for yourself if you have three dollars to spare. That's what it costs to spend *La Siesta* at Rosalinda's."

Longarm smiled dubiously and replied, "I dunno, that's a lot of *dinero* for an afternoon flop, ain't it?"

Greek Steve laughed and said, "It sure is. It's a good thing we don't get to town that often. But whenever we do, three dollars ain't such bad value for a whole afternoon at Rosalinda's.

Longarm smiled sheepishy and confessed he'd been slow at arithmetic as a schoolboy, too. Then he said, "You gents go on and . . . cool off all you like. I'm really looking for a job and I have to husband my pocket jingle until I get one."

Chongo insisted, "Come on, Crawford. I'll put in a word for you at Rosalinda's. I'll ask Miss Connie about you, too, the next time I see her. You did say you know how to rope and throw, didn't you?"

Longarm gathered up his gear as he replied in a disgusted tone, "What does rope and throw mean, Mister? I just got out west from a finishing school for young ladies and I've never been too clear about which end of the bull the bullshit comes out of."

So the three of them headed down the way to a thick-walled 'dobe wrapped around a shady patio with no windows facing the sun-baked streets of Sheffield-Crossing. Longarm knew before he could see the house of ill repute that Chongo was aiming to fix him up with a local gal paid extra to pump a strange rider's mind as she took care of his carnal needs.

He didn't care. He could lie just as swell to anyone and, after all that time by rail and trail since he'd parted with Miss Bubbles, his needs were commencing to hurt.

Thick 'dobe walls were popular with everybody in West Texas who knew what was good for them. By warming and cooling way slower than wood frame or even baked bricks, adobe tended to even things out, indoors, betwixt the scorching sunny days and the cold starry nights of the usually cloudless Southwest. The patio's lily pond, shaded by fig trees and a big old weeping willow, had it close to ten degrees cooler off the streets of Sheffield-Crossing. It seemed even cooler in the dark cavernous tap-room beyond, where earlier arrivals lounged with the mostly Mex gals who worked there. The few that didn't look Mex seemed more colored or pure Indian. One was either Chinee or that odd blend of blood lines the Mexicans themselves called "Chino." All of 'em were a tad younger and prettier than the average soiled dove in an Anglo whorehouse of the day. Latin gals in general took up whoring with less pissing, moaning, and strong drink. So they tended to offer a greater selection to choose from and some of them even seemed to enjoy their work.

Chongo and Greek Steve led Longarm over to the corner bar and introduced him as their old pal, Duncan Crawford. Then Chongo allowed he'd be back as soon as he had a word with Madam Rosalinda, her fat self. So Longarm and the cooled-off Greek Steve had their tequila in the border manner, with a lick of salt and a lemon-half chaser. It was fair tequila. The gal tending bar in her chemise insisted they gaze on the clear glass bottle she'd poured from, anyhow. She seemed proud to work in such a high-toned place. Longarm agreed that pickled worm bobbing around in the genuine tequila proved her point, even if it would have been easy enough to drop a maguey worm in a bottle full of grain spirits, as was often the case down Mexico way, where only a hundred proof, distilled from maguey or century plant, was supposed to be sold as tequila. Longarm had often wondered how there'd be enough worms to go around, boring through the average maguey heart.

Chongo soon rejoined them, along with that pretty whore with Chino features, wearing no more than a thin silk chemise that barely covered half her shapely sallow thighs. Her raven's-wing hair was cut sort of short and worn in bangs, Chinee or perhaps Apache Style.

She never looked higher than Longarm's fly as Chongo introduced her as Miss Perfidia and added, "She says she don't take it Greek Style. So, I reckon she's with you, Crawford."

Greek Steve muttered, "Fuck you!" into his tequila.

The oddly oriental looking Mex gal smiled shyly without meeting his eyes and asked, "*¿Habla 'spañol, Querido?*"

To which Longarm felt it best to reply, "*Muy poco*, ma'am. We're in Texas, now. We'll get along better if you can manage Texas talk."

She shrugged her bare shoulders and said, "*Yo comrendo.* You wish for to fuck me instead of for to *chinge* me, *correcto*?"

Longarm laughed, allowed that was about the size of it and drained his stemmed glass of tequila to follow her upstairs where it was even cooler. He would have been more hesitant if he hadn't been able to tell his nagging conscience that bedding a whore in the line of duty, free, wasn't the same as patronizing a whorehouse like a simp. The way she swung that shapely behind under one layer of thin silk as she strode up the stairs and down the hall ahead of him made his sacrifice seem a tad easier to contemplate. He knew she was walking that way on purpose. It sure beat all how Mexicans named gals Dolores, Perfidia, and such. You hardly ever met Anglo gals named Sadness or Astray. This strayed slanty-eyed one had likely changed her name for business reasons, like Silver Heels, Snake Hips, or Squirrel Tooth in more Anglo houses of ill repute.

The chamber Perfidia led him too was small and dark enough to qualify for a nun's cell. There was even a grimly realistic crucifix nailed to the 'dobe wall above the head of the bed. But after that the bed was a tad bigger and softer than you'd find in most convents and the window slit was glazed with rose colored panes to make everything inside look sort of like fresh meat.

As she shut and barred the door behind them Perfidia said, *"Bueno!* We are free to talk, now. For why have you come to Sheffield-Crossing, *Querido*? Do you search for *Don David El Diablo*? Those rangers who came by told us they were seeking, too."

Longarm said, "I don't know who you're talking about and I'm only a poor but honest cow hand, looking for a damned job. Who's this Diablo gent and do you want to fuck or gossip?"

Perfidia laughed girlishly and said, *"Si, ahora mismo,"* in a casual tone, considering the way she peeled her chemise off over her head to face him bold as brass without a stitch.

Her tawny torso betrayed some European ancestry by curving in and out more than Indian or Oriental shapes that short usually managed.

But like many Indian or Oriental gals, Perfidia sported way less body hair than your average white gal and Longarm's needs grew one hell of a lot more urgent when she calmly sat down on the bed covers, leaned back on her elbows to spread her thighs wide as she raised her bare feet from the floor.

He made a point of hanging his sixgun handy on a bedpost and draping his duds neatly over the one chair and it's rail back as he undressed casually enough to prove he wasn't an eager kid with an uncontrollable hard-on. He did have a hard-on and he suspected he was only showboating as a smooth Don Juan for himself. For despite all the bullshit about how you were supposed to treat ladies like whores and whores like ladies he knew most gals, even schoolmarms, knew way more about men than they let on. For whether a young gal wanted to study men or not, men commenced to study gals and make total assholes out of themselves long before young gals were allowed to receive flowers, books, and candy from any of 'em.

So, knowing how dumb it was to walk a picket fence for a schoolgal or pretend you were in charge to a whore, Longarm rose from that chair in his own naked glory, stiff as a poker, to move over to the bed and take Perfidia up on her kind offer.

Her slant eyes opened wide and she gasped, "*Ay, que grueso!*" as he dropped to his knees on the rug to enter her, pleasantly surprised by her tightly pulsating, wet warmth, even before she began to move her hips in time with his thrusts. He found himself really thrusting, after all that time without a woman. It felt sort of silly to enjoy even a pretty whore that much. But she was one hell of a lay, and he was sort of proud of himself for not proposing to take her away from all this and make her his own forever by the time he'd come in her hard enough to feel it all the way down to his clenched toes.

If he hadn't known better, he'd have believed her when she moaned she'd come, too. Neither one of them felt all that cool, now. So when she suggested they get into a less awkward position to smoke and sip sangria, Longarm allowed that sounded like a swell notion.

But she didn't seem to have a pitcher of wine punch on hand, and it got even less comfortable when, after she'd let him light them a cheroot to share as they leaned against the headboard side by side, Perfidia suddenly said, "*Bueno*. Now tell me what it is you really want here in Sheffield-Crossing and my other friends and I will help you all we can."

Longarm blew smoke out both nostrils like a pissed-off bull and told her, "I don't know what you're talking about. You seem to have me mixed up with somebody else."

58

She began to toy with his limp organ grinder as she sighed amorously and said, "I do not have you mixed up with someone else. I knew as soon as you took your *pantalones* off you had to be *El Brazo Largo*!"

Chapter 8

It didn't work. Longarm took a thoughtful drag on his cheroot, blew a smoke ring, and tried to sound only mildly confounded when he said, "I told you I don't speak much Mex. Are you complaining about my old organ grinder being too bulky or my arms being too long? You should have said so if I was hurting you, just now."

She commenced to fondle his dong more fondly as she insisted, "I was not certain until you had this in me. Then I was. The *muchacha* who pointed you out to me in San Antonio said it came in her eight times in one night!"

He didn't bite. He blew another smoke ring and said, "She must have been might pretty. Or she was surely out to flatter this rascal you mistake me for. You say they call him *El Brazo Largo* in San Antone?"

She sighed and said, "Is San *Antonio*, no matter what you Americanos say, and we both know *El Brazo Largo* is more famous south of the border.

He pretended to yawn, patted her bare shoulder with his free hand and answered, "How come, and don't stop doing just what you're doing, Miss Perfidia."

She began to stroke his half swollen member faster as she insisted, "We both know for why. But if this is some sort of test, we both know how those *ladrones* stole our *revolución*

61

when our Benito Juarez died. We both know how the people have suffered under *El Presidente* Diaz and how some patriots from the high-born *El Gato* to a woman of the fields called La Mariposa wage *La Guerrilla* against his cruel *Federales* and even worse *Rurales*!"

Longarm suggested, "Why don't you roll over and let me shove this to you dog style? It's warming up in here and dog style would be way cooler. I've never been able to keep up with all that feuding back and forth down Mexico way. Like I said, my Spanish is limited and sometimes I doubt your countrymen, themselves, know what in blue blazes they might be fighting about, no offense."

She let go of his re-inspired erection to roll on her hands and knees as he asked, even whilst she pouted, "I am most pained that you will not trust me! My only desire is for to help! I would be honored to be able to say I once helped *El Brazo Largo Famoso*!"

Longarm rose with one knee on the sheet betwixt her brown calves as he braced the other foot on the floor to take a dusky hemisphere of shapely ass in either extended palm to let his old organ grinder find its own way as he assured her, "You're helping this wayfaring stranger get through this siesta just fine and, in days to come, there's nothing to stop you from saying you came eight times with this nine-day wonder you have me confounded with. You have my word I've never tried to overthrow the recognized government of Mexico."

She reached down to guide the head inside and stroke his balls for encouragement as she insisted with a cheek of her *face* on a pillow. "Nobody ever said you had, except those unjust *Rurales* who became so enraged when you simply refused for to let them rob and rape while you were riding through, after some of your own *banditos*. I know who you are after, here in Sheffield-Crossing! Why won't you let me and my own friends help you?"

He assured her she was helping him relax a heap, after over a week without any. He added, sincerely, "I was getting horny enough to do this to a real dog, or an ugly woman, least ways. I never dreamed I was saving this up for a gal as friendly and pretty as you, Miss Perfidia!''

She arched her spine and moaned, "*Ay, que hermoso!* I am enjoying it, too! You may not believe this, but there are times I do not enjoy this at all with a *parroquiano.*"

He shoved teasingly and allowed he doubted he'd enjoy it with a parrot, either. He pretended not to get it when she laughed like hell. It made her innards ripple swell around his shaft and there'd have been no jest at all if he'd admitted he'd understood her to mean there were times she didn't enjoy it with a *customer.*

From the way she was offering up her sweet meat Longarm doubted the warm-natured little gal hated it all that often with most anybody. They all *said* they were only in the trade for the money, and there had to be some customers who really disgusted them. But for all their talk about men being beasts and their having no other way to make a living, whores bragged on who they would and wouldn't service and it only stood to reason that a self-respecting whore who didn't enjoy fucking at least as much as a top hand enjoyed riding would settle for some other line of work, like waiting tables or minding kids for rich ladies.

He rolled her on her back to finish right with that pillow under her rolicking rump and her tawny legs wrapped around his waist whilst he found himself kissing her, to his mingled surprise and distaste. It sure beat all how a man could walk the straight and narrow for days at a time and then wind up wallowing in sin and degradation like that Ben Hur in Governor Wallace's book, enjoying every vile wriggle and jiggle.

They wound up with her on top, sobbing about how he'd ruined her for any other customers that evening whilst he sucked a nipple and shot yet another wad up into her. Then she said she'd go fetch them that sangria at last, and he was too spent and too thirsty to do anything but lie there sweaty and too out of breath to want another smoke or, hell, anything at all, for the foreseeable future.

63

Some kindly old philospher had written, doubtless in French, that the only times a man was completely sane was after a good lay. Longarm proved his point as soon as Perfidia was back in her chemise and out in the hall, by rolling out of bed to get the double derringer from his denim jacket and flop back in bed with the wicked little weapon in hand under the sheet he'd draped modestly over his privates.

Down in the kitchen, the fully dressed Chongo loomed out of the shadows to demand, *"Que tal? Hay algo para mi?"*

Perfidia replied in a desperately casual tone, *"No se preocupe.* He knows for how to treat a woman, but he is nobody important. They would not send a *diputado federale* here alone who did not speak more Spanish than that one, eh?"

Chongo growled, "He could be pretending to know less than he lets on about everything."

The pretty whore fluttered her lashes and smiled knowingly as she assured Chongo, "He does not speak much Spanish. There are ways for a working girl to test a man when he is at his most *maravilloso* in her. I tested him with other surprise questions. I am sure he knows little or nothing about anyone around here or any problems they might be having. I told him I'd come down here for to get some sangria. It is starting to get *muy caliente* and the wine may get him for to tell me more. But I am certain he is no more than a wandering *vaquero Yanqui* looking for work."

So Chongo told her she was doing swell, patted her on her rump, and let her pass to fetch the sangria.

Sangria translated literally as "bloodshed," but Mexicans as often meant a cooling summer drink made from citrus and other fruit juices with red wine, ice, and tequila if there was either handy. It looked more like cherry punch than blood and tasted . . . well, like sangria. Few folk who got to drink any sangria on a hot West Texas day ever complained about the taste and the kick could make your world seem a better place, made with enough tequila.

Perfidia carried a pitcher made with enough tequila back up to her room as she considered the lack of trust shown by *El Brazo Largo*. As a woman who made a good living understanding men, Perfidia had figured out why he wouldn't trust a strange woman he'd just met, no matter how many times he might come in her. As a patriotic Mexican despite her social position, or perhaps because of it, Perfidia still wanted to help. So she'd decided on the best way by the time she was back in bed with him, serving him sangria and anything else he might desire as she pretended he had her fooled.

She'd lied to Chongo about a truer friend of her people because he rode for the *grandeza* Consuela Deveruex y Lopez and anyone could see a famous *diputado federale* had to be after that worthless *mierdito* of a brother she was trying for to save again. Like many another in the lower Pecos Valley, Perfidia was more afraid of the powerful Deveruex-Lopez clan than anxious to save a homicidal lunatic indulged by his family as if he'd been no worse than a spoiled brat. But neither the really friendly whore nor any of her real friends knew where David El Diablo might be hiding, or whether he was even back on his home range after that daring escape up north. So perhaps it didn't really matter that *El Brazo Largo* only wanted to sip sangria and have sex with her. She could still help him in other ways, in spite of himself.

Chongo had ordered her to find out more about this Duncan Crawford *El Brazo Largo* claimed to be. If she asked him what she was supposed to tell Chongo, *El Brazo Largo* would just try to change the subject again, and it was getting too hot for to *chingar*.

So she snuggled closer, running her iced glass over his hairy belly to comfort him as she coyly pumped her bedmate as if she believed in the tooth fairy and a saddle tramp called Duncan Crawford, Sweet *Santa Maria, Madre de Dios!*

She found her *siesta* sharer more willing to gossip about the range he'd been riding up New Mexico way. Longarm has passed through a lot of it on more than one field mission. That was one of the main reasons he'd decided on being an out-of-work New Mexico rider. He was on safe ground saying the late Major Murphy's big store in Lincoln had been converted to the county court house, or that Dad Peppin had resigned as Sheriff, with the easy-going George Kimbrell filling in Dad Peppin's unexpired term until the coming November elections.

Being a woman, Perfidia wanted to hear more about the scandalous carryings on betwixt Uncle John Chisum and his so-called niece, over Roswell way at South Spring, and, again, Longarm was on safe ground for bullshitting because he'd been there, more than once, if not as Duncan Crawford.

He truthfully told the Texas whore, "Miss Sally behaved as a warm and hospitable lady when they coffeed and caked me at South Spring. I know some say she's the daughter of Uncle John's dead brother, James, whilst others say she's just a young play-pretty a man going on sixty would feel silly marrying up with. I don't know whether it's true he sleeps on the floor in a bedroll at night, neither. The main house was furnished luxurious and Miss Sally had manners fit for Queen Victoria's court the few times I dropped by. Chisum's made a heap of friends and enemies grazing all them Jingle Bob and Long Rail cows up yonder. All them newspaper reporters filling in the blanks of that Lincoln County War has added to the mythology. I can tell you for a fact that nobody on either side gunned a bunch of Chisum riders and inspired Uncle John to switch sides. He pulled in his horns when the gunplay got serious, the same as everyone else with a lick of sense. Before you ask, this child never rode for either side. I'm a cow hand, not a gun hand."

She assured him she believed him and so, what with some more smoking and sipping, with her indulging in a little sucking, they passed away the smouldering heat of a West Texas day, and when the *siesta* hours had ended and he asked how much he owed her, she blubbered up and ran out of the room crying, holding the hem of her chemise to her eyes with a hell of a view exposed. So Longarm got dressed and left to

66

find some place he could bed down more serious for the coming night.

Nobody with a lick of sense rode clean across the country by coach, now that you could ride by rail from New York to San Francisco. But the rebel state of Texas had been left behind at railroad building because of the war and the longer Reconstruction that had followed. So they still had a stage line running betwixt San Antone and El Paso, with a spur line up and down the Pecos to feed mail and passengers to the same.

That gave Sheffield-Crossing its own station, where a body could stay overnight if he wanted to. So Longarm hired a cell smaller than Perfidia's, with a cot a monk or nun might find a tad narrow, and left his saddlebags there with his Winchester so's he could make it to the *Paseo* in the church plaza they'd be starting just after sundown.

Paseo hailed from a Spanish verb that covered gaping, loitering, or strolling aimless. As *El Paseo*, it covered a more thought-out way to stretch one's legs betwixt the afternoon siesta and the late-night suppers most Spanish-speaking folk went in for, once it got cool enough to slurp hot soup, and, for all the mean things some Texicans had to say about Mexicans, they'd taken to *El Paseo* in West Texas the same as they'd taken to Mex boots, saddles, sombreros, and other such greaser notions that only made common sense in hot dry cow country.

Every town that had at least one Papist church had a plaza, and it was up to the ladies of the town whether they wanted to circle it clockwise or the other way as they worked up an appetite for supper or whatever in their evening outfits, which were generally fandango skirts and off-the-shoulder blouses, in border country.

The gents of the town strolled around the plaza counter to the she-male flow as the sun went down and lanterns were lit to make everybody look more interesting. You could hardly tell if a couple of gigglesome gals coming your way needed a bath or not as you passed each other, not looking, the first time or so. After you passed the same gal *more* times, it was considered only natural to ogle anyone so fine. It was up to her whether she ogled or even smiled back. Once you got to smiling at one another in passing it was considered all right to ask her how she felt about joining you later for supper or whatever. Her menfolk were not required to kill you for the family honor if she'd met you at *El Paseo*, where any unescorted shemale was on her own. Big brothers who really cared just forbade their sister to go to the plaza. And so hardly anyone but Anglos ever got hurt. Hard-up Mexicans didn't get humiliated by gals who might not fancy them because they never spoke to the gal until she'd sent the proper smoke signals with her eyes. It was the overly anxious Anglo boys who tended to fresh-mouth a gal who'd just looked clean through them.

When Longarm got to the plaza, things were just getting started as a couple of really dreadful-looking young gals strolled alone, counterclockwise, in the soft light of gloaming.

Longarm took up a position under a street lantern and lit a smoke as he waited to see what might happen next. The last thing he wanted at the moment was a start-from-scratch with another Mexican gal. But a stranger sizing up the local action looked less suspicious than a stranger starting conversations in saloons and barber shops.

So what happened next was Chongo. The branding crew boss sidled up to Longarm, smoking his own brand, to say, "*Buenoches*. Didn't you get enough pussy this afternoon, old son?"

Longarm shrugged and said, "Thanks to you. I owe you a swell piece of ass, but I'm sorry to say I don't bend over for other boys. What might you be doing here, if you don't want either of them ugly young gals out yonder?"

Chongo said, "Miss Connie Deveruex sent me to fetch you. She and her momma, Dona Felicidad, are expecting you for supper. Take my well-meant advice and accept her kind invitation."

Chapter 9

Their town house was just to the other side of the church, Chongo told Longarm along the way, because old Dona Felicidad spent so much of her time with her rosary in the family pew these days. Her daughter had bought her the town house after she'd been widowed and taken to pining alone out to their homespread down the valley.

Longarm knew before they got there that the supper invite was just a white lie. It wasn't right eight o'clock yet, and high-toned Hispanics were inclined to dine at nine or ten and stay up way past Anglo bedtime, to put in the usual amount of sleep humans needed, in two four-hour shifts. One in the wee small hours and the other during the *siesta* hours just past. You could get four hours of sleep when you didn't spend a *siesta* with someone like Perfidia.

A gatekeeper in livery and a Schofield .45 let them into a fancier patio than Rosalinda's, and Rosalinda's patio was fancier than most. The moorish-tiled fountain sported running water, meaning someone had to pump well water to a roof tank now and again. Most big Hispanic houses had more help hanging about than they really needed. Travel writers who low-rated the pitiful salaries paid to Mex household help missed the point that, like some Indians who kept extra wives,

Mexican *patrones* were expected to take on kith and kin who had no place else to be.

So there was a butler in livery to let them into the grand entrance across the patio and an Indian gal dressed like a French maid to lead them into the main *sala*, where that dusky blonde Longarm had already seen sat by a cold baronial fireplace with an older, once pretty lady with a darker complexion but likely some white blood. .They'd both dressed for supper in black gowns and mantillas with Spanish lace to crown their gold and silver heads, respective. It wasn't clear to Longarm whether they were in mourning for that dead *vaquero*, the late head of their house, or just dressed hightoned. Hispanic blue-bloods tended to dress sort of gloomy as well as expensive, in velvet or lace to match a coal bin at midnight.

Consuela Deveruex y Lopez looked more imperious up close than she had trudging down the street behind that hearse, and she hadn't trudged all that humble to begin with. When Chongo introduced Longarm to her as Duncan Crawford she held out the back of her hand to say, *"Ay, si, un nombre escocea. Esta Usted en su casa."* Then she caught Longarm's deliberately dumb expression and added, *"¿No habla Usted Español?"*

Longarm shook with her instead of kissing her hand as he sheepishly replied, "I got that last part, ma'am. I can talk enough Mex to get in trouble. But most of the words I know in the lingo ain't fit for the ears of such fine ladies."

So she told him in plain English to set a spell because supper wasn't ready yet. He noticed Chongo leaving as he sat down across from them in one of those straight-back Spanish chairs designed for sitting up prim and proper. The dusky blonde and her confused-looking mother had the more comfortable-looking sofa to themselves.

Devil Dave's older sister was about the same height as the mean little shit, making her taller than average for a gal. Her English was as natural and a tad more refined than his own. Longarm wondered idly whether her kind felt more Tex or

Mex most of the time. There were a lot of her kind in West Texas and even more up New Mexico way these days.

Still another maid came in to serve them all red wine with cheese and tortillas. The daughter of the house said he had their permit to smoke if he liked. When Longarm allowed he was trying to cut down on tobacco, she suddenly blurted, "Chongo tells us you said you'd ridden for a Diamond K in *New Mexico*?"

Longarm had already had time to reconsider that whopper. So he met her eye and smiled easily as he explained, "That ain't exactly what I said, ma'am. Leastways, it wasn't exactly what I meant. Diamond K was the trail brand on some ponies I rode herd on betwixt Fort Union and Roswell. I can't tell you where that remuda started out from."

She said, "I can. The Diamond K is a horse-breeding spread south of Denver, Colorado. You say you only signed on at Fort Union?"

Longarm washed down some tortilla-wrapped cheese with the mighty fine dry wine and replied, "A couple of hands had quit along the way. I'd just run some army beef up to Fort Union and—"

"Do you know *El Cabrito*?" she suddenly cut in, to his considerable relief. But he made himself sound slightly pissed as he soberly replied, "If you mean that wild youth some of your folk translate *El Cabrito* or *Chivito* from The Kid, I sure wish you'd tell me why everybody asks me that the minute I say I hail from New Mexico territory. I hate to brag, but I do ride Top Hand, which is more than any Henry McCarty, William Bonney, Kid Antrim, or Billy The Kid can say. He may be handy with a shovel or gun. Such fame as he deserves comes from his having outlived most of the gun hands of the Chisum, Tunstall, McSween side. He was riding under the late Dick Brewer and taking his orders from Lawyer McSween during most of that religious argument, Miss Connie."

The dusky blonde blinked and allowed she'd never heard the Lincoln County War described as a religious argument before.

71

Longarm shrugged and replied, "There wasn't much else for grown men to get so wild about, Miss Connie. The whole sorry mess lasted a mere six months and left the leaders on both sides dead or a lot less prosperous than they'd started out."

He sipped some wine and continued, "On the one side was Major L.G. Murphy, Jim Dolan, and Sheriff Bill Brady, Irish Catholics who'd got there first. The side favored by a mostly Protestant national press were either out to break a business-ranching monopoly or horn in on a mostly Catholic Tex-Mex community, depending on who you ask. They were funded by their rich Uncle John Chisum. Stockman Hank Tunstall and a side-switching Lawyer McSween set up their own general store, hotel, and bank across the street from the Murphy-Dolan premises in Lincoln. Chisum, Tunstall, and McSween were a mixed bag of Protestants. So the Irish Catholic Sheriff Brady sided with Murphy and Dolan and the fun and games began."

She frowned thoughtfully and said, "I was told The Kid followed our own *Santa Fe* and gets on well with Mexicans."

Longarm shrugged and said, "You're speaking of a teen-ager who doesn't spend much time in any church. A heap that's been written about his earlier boyhood seems to be total twaddle. He started out riding for Jim Dolan. He changed jobs and sides when Hank Tunstall's foreman, Dick Brewer, made him a better offer. Despite what's been said about him aveng-ing the death of a man who'd been a father to him, The Kid had been on Tunstall's payroll three weeks when Sheriff Brady's deputies shot old Hank in February of '78. Brady got shot in the back in April. A few days later Buckshot Roberts and Dick Brewer killed each other in the same shoot-out. By July the Murphy-Dolan faction had their new sheriff, Dad Peppin, surround the McSween-Tunstall property across the street from them and burn it out, killing McSween and four or five others to end the so-called war, six months after in began, with both sides ruined and hardly anybody hiring since. That's why I ain't still up yonder, riding for anybody."

The old lady suddenly jumped up to run from the room as if she had the trots. She was gone before her daughter and Longarm could rise politely. Connie said, "You must excuse my mother. She doesn't speak English and she hasn't been well lately."

Longarm allowed most folk found the Lincoln County War tedious in any lingo. She said she had a morbid interest in young gunfighters and asked what he'd heard about her family problem.

He said he'd heard her dad had died and left her in charge of things.

"Nothing about my younger brother, David?" she insisted.

He made himself go through the motions of trying to remember before he brightened and tried, "Oh, was that your brother that Texas Ranger was asking me about, earlier? He did ask me whether I knew some local boy called Devilish Dave and I told him true I had no idea where such an oddly described cuss might be found. You say Devilish Dave is your kid brother, Miss Connie? How come they call him Devilish Dave?"

She sighed and said, "They don't. They call him Devil Dave Deveruex and I fear he has some . . . mental condition. He had a bad bout of scarlet fever when we were little. They say that can leave a body . . . touched."

Longarm allowed he's heard as much and didn't press her to explain further. He knew exactly how crazy-mean Devil Dave was. The reasons he preferred the owlhoot trail to running the family business were moot, as far as that murder warrant signed by Judge Dickerson read.

He tried to change the subject before she could ask him something he might not be set for. He said, "To tell the pure truth I was way more interested in something else they told me about you, Miss Connie. They said you were fixing to drive some beef to market and I couldn't help noticing you'd lost one of your regular riders."

She nodded absently and said, "Jesus Robles. He was a good man but a poor rider. I shall be driving a few hundred head to the railhead at San Antonio in a few days. If you're asking for a job, I fear I have all the help I need at the moment. Do you know how much it costs to hire a professional gunfighter, such as Billy The Kid?''

As a lawman, Longarm did. Five-hundred dollars a month was the going price for a gun hand willing to kill most anybody for you, while you could hire a bodyguard way cheaper. Bodyguards hardly ever got hung for gunning paid assassins. He said, ''I've no idea what Billy The Kid was paid by John Tunstall the one payday he got anything. Lawyer McSween swore Dick Brewer, Billy, and others in as private range detectives and they called themselves Regulators for all of three or four weeks before the county told them they couldn't. I suspect that you could hire The Kid right cheap, right now, Miss Connie. But I don't know where he is, and anybody else who did might just as willingly turn him in for the price on his head. I think it was over a hundred dollars, the last time I'd heard.''

She said, ''I don't want to hire any young killers. I only wish I knew what made them like that. My brother, David, has gotten in with bad company. We've tried to calm him more than once. A lawyer we'd sent to help him just wound up dead in another silly shootout! It wasn't David who shot his own lawyer. It was one of those crazy-mean breeds he's been riding with since our father died!''

Longarm knew he'd better flutter away from the candle flame before he burned his wings by showing too much interest. He could see how upset she was in spite of her calm outside. Worries were running around in those big brown eyes like trapped rats dying to bust out. He sipped the last of his wine, set the glass down next to some cheese he hadn't eaten, and quietly asked, ''Do you mind if I make a personal observation, ma'am?''

She dimpled at him to ask what he had in mind.

He said, ''You're looking poorly, no offense. I can't tell what you might be coming down with. But if you ain't coming down with something you have too much on your mind to cope with the likes of me tonight. Your momma was upset about something, too. So why don't we call off that supper invite and set you both free to deal with whatever might be ailing the two of you?''

She stared owl-eyed to demand, hopefully, ''Do you mean that? Are you sure you won't feel insulted?''

He got to his feet, hat in hand, to reply with a sporting smile. ''There's nothing to get sore about, ma'am. You ladies invited me over for supper before something else came up and unsettled you. If I eat somewhere's else this evening I'm no worse off than I would have been to begin with.''

She rose, too, saying, ''But I feel so awkward, sending for you, only to send you away with nothing!''

He said, ''I enjoyed that wine tremendous, and the cheese wasn't half bad, ma'am. So I got more out of you than you got out of me. I'm sorry I ain't the gun hand you may have took me for, Miss Connie. That's just the way things go sometimes.''

She gasped, ''Good heavens! Did you think I wanted to hire you as a gunfighter, ah, Duncan?''

He said, ''We've established you ain't hiring at all, Miss Connie. It's been nice talking to you. But I reckon I'd best get it on down the road, and I sure hope you and your momma get to feeling better real soon, hear?''

She didn't argue further. She led him part way and then that butler showed him out the front gate to the *calle*. It was still early, and the *paseo* tended to get more interesting near the end, as couples paired off after all that strolling and smirking. He still felt no great awakening in his loins, thanks to good old Perfidia, but the more a stranger showed his face around a small town the less strange it got.

So Longarm circled the big church to get back to the plaza, cutting through the graveyard, shaded night and day by ancient blackjack oaks. As he did so a Mex in a *charro* outfit, big sombrero, and a brace of Remington sixguns stepped out of a side door of the church rectory. Longarm dismissed him as likely a pal of that D Bar L rider they'd buried earlier that same day. The Mex was headed his way, away from the plaza and *El Paseo* as if heading home for his own late supper. So Longarm nodded as they met in a puddle of lamplight and then, just as Longarm murmured, "*Buenoches*," the strange Mex grabbed for both his sixguns, gasping, "*Ay, caramba! No es posible!*"

He might have caught Longarm more off guard if he'd slapped leather without yelling like that. But he had yelled, and so Longarm got his own gun out and threw down as the both of them fired.

Hot lead whipped by Longarm's shoulders on either side as his own two hundred grains of the same split the other man's breast bone and chewed up the heart inside.

Then Longarm was off the path and waist deep in tombstones whilst the stranger he'd shot flopped like a hauled-in trout in a spreading pool of blood, with his hat and guns farflung on the brick pavement.

As Longarm reloaded a distant voice called out, "*¿A 'onde, que pasa?*"

He yelled back, "*¡Aqui! ¡Quiero ver al policia!*"

So there he was when an older Anglo lawman wearing a pewter star came tearing along the path with his own gun drawn, saw Longarm, and called out in English, "What's up? Do you know who fired all them shots just now, stranger?"

Longarm soberly replied. I fired one of 'em. I'm still working on why this dead cuss over here fired the others. I'd be Duncan Crawford out of New Mexico Territory. I've no idea who *he* might have been."

The town law moved closer, nudged the limp body with his boot tip, and said, "Whoever he was, you surely cleaned his plow. So I'm asking you, polite, to hand over that sixgun and come along with me."

Chapter 10

Longarm saw no better course than to comply. He still had his ace-in-the-hole double derringer, and if push came to shove he could still tell them who he really was. The grave-yard was crowding some as he got back on the path and surrendered his sixgun. He'd just told the old coot he'd fired the blamed weapon. But the town law sniffed at the muzzle anyhow. They'd likely stolen him away from Scotland Yard.

He had enough sense to wave some Mex kids back as an even older man of the cloth came out that same rectory door. He turned out to be their priest. When he saw what Longarm had wrought he knelt by the body to see if Extreme Unction might help. Longarm got the town law to wait until the priest had finished his Pater Noster before he respectfully said, "He was out to kill me. He came out of your rectory just now, Padre."

The elderly Mex priest looked up at them, confused, to reply, "I do not know this *pobrecito*. He looks like an *Indio puro*. You say he was inside our *rectorio* earlier?"

Longarm said, "He must have been. That's where he was coming from when we met in this path, I howdied him, and he went for his guns. Is it possible he was wandering about, inside, without you folk knowing?"

The priest bent lower for a better look at the dead man in

77

the dim light before he decided. "I have never seen him before. He must have hidden in the church beyond until after vespers. A door from behind the altar is not locked. If he hid in one of the pews until after we held our evening services . . . But for why? We are a poor parish. There is nothing worth stealing anywhere on the *premisas!*"

Longarm felt better about the old gun sniffer when he told the priest, "He was likely hiding from this ranger who's come to town, looking for the Deveruex boy and some Mexican pals. He might have mistook this other stranger for that ranger, just now. They don't look alike. But they're both Anglo strangers, and you know what they say about a guilty conscience."

The lawman called two kids out of the crowd to say, "Pancho, I want you to go fetch Doc Waterford and tell him the county has a dead body for him to gather, here. Manuel, I want you to run over to my office and tell 'em I need some help, here."

As they were sorting that out Longarm quietly asked the priest if he knew Devil Dave Deveruex.

The older man sighed and said, "He was one of our altar boys before he went astray. But, alas, he has not been to Mass or Confession since he seems to have gone *loco en la cabeza!*"

The older lawman opined, "He likely doesn't care to confess what he's been up to." Let's get going, Mister Crawford."

Longarm asked, "Don't you reckon we ought to wait until them other gents you sent for get here?"

The old timer asked, "Are you trying to tell me how to do this job? Are you some sort of lawman your ownself?"

Longarm shrugged and said, "I reckon you know the folk in your own town better than I do. Makes no nevermind to me if they steal this dead bird's boots and guns."

He turned as if to head back to the center of town. The old timer with the pewter badge said, "Hold on. We'd best wait 'til some of our junior deputies get here to watch that big hat, too.''

Then, as if to recover lost ground, he added, ''It's still up to our deputy coroner, Doc Waterford, to go through the rascal's pockets and figure out who he might have been, hear?''

So they waited a spell and the town law accepted one of Longarm's cheroots as folk from all over town gathered a respectful distance to crane for a view through the trunks and inky shadows of the blackjacks.

Travis of the Texas Rangers arrived with a couple of other Anglo lawmen from the town marshal's office. He had the sense to address a man he knew to be a federal deputy as Mister Crawford.

The older town law holding Longarm and his gun asked, ''You know this gent, Ranger Travis?''

The younger Texican said, ''Talked to him earlier. Checked out his story by wire. New Mexico Territory has him down as a poor but honest rider who's not wanted for nothing, as far as they can recall. What's he done here in Sheffield-Crossing?''

The town law grudgingly told the ranger, ''Just shot him a more mysterious Mex. It's commencing to look as if he was telling the truth about that, too.''

Travis moved closer, spied the sprawled body, and hunkered down for a closer look, striking a match to make sure before he said, ''I could swear this was Hernando Nana, Mission Apache and known associate of Devil Dave Deveruex. He just escaped from the law up Colorado way with pals believed to be Nana and a breed of some kind called Hogan. Another pal called Ramon Kayitah got killed by that famous Longarm during the bustout.''

Longarm saw Chongo and some other D Bar L riders in the crowd as the older town law told Travis, ''I've heard tell of that federal rider they call Longarm. Have you ever met up with him, Ranger Travis?''

The ranger looked as if butter wouldn't melt in his mouth whilst he rose right next to Longarm to shake out his match and soberly say, "I have. Worked with him one time along the border. Sometimes he acts like his shit don't stink. But he ain't a bad tracker."

The town's deputy coroner arrived with some of his own help to crowd around the town law above the remains. So Travis was able to edge Longarm into the shadows a mite and mutter, "What the fuck is going on, old pard?"

Longarm said, "I wish I knew. I never got a look at the pals shooting up Devil Dave's trial. If you're right about that being one of them I overestimated their brains a heap. They must have beelined for here whilst I was pussyfooting in, so smart. Nana, there, must have looked us all over some before they started shooting up that courtroom. It's the only way he could have recognized me at a glance, in this light, in a different outfit. That's one of the prices of being famous, I reckon."

Travis asked how he wanted to play the next hand.

Longarm murmured, "Close to the vest. If the man I want made it here ahead of me it's still up for grabs where he's holed up and who might be aiding and abetting him. I just came from the Deveruex-Lopez town house. If his mother and sister have him hidden in their pantry, they're better actresses than most. I suspect the sister was feeling me out as a gun hand. What can you tell me about her errand boy, Chongo?"

The ranger said, "Anglo-Mex boss wrangler out at her spread. Has to know horses and gets along better with 'em than any of the other crew bosses. She seems to regard him as a sort of pet ape because he cared for her and her ponies when she was little. Courting her would be above old Chongo's station, but don't ever insult her if Chongo's within ear-shot. Why are we talking about such a tedious asshole?"

Longarm said, "I ain't sure, yet. I ain't figured out whether he's a pal of Devil Dave or worried Devil Dave will come pestering his boss-lady some more. I can't complain about the way he's been feeling me out, so far. Might you rangers have any Greek outlaws on your wanted fliers?"

Travis blinked and asked, "Should we?"

Longarm said, "I told Chongo you'd asked me about some Greek on the run, earlier in that saloon. I didn't want to tell him what we were really talking about."

So the ranger chuckled and decided, "As I recall our conversation, I asked you who you were and whether you'd ever met up with a Greek outlaw called . . . How about Plato? Wasn't Plato some sort of famous Greek outlaw?"

Longarm said, "Close enough. He made some shocking suggestions as to who might do what to whom with his old organ grinder. Might be safer to tell anyone who asks that what you ask other gents is none of their business as long as you don't make an outright liar out of me."

The ranger said he'd try not to, but added, "You know it's only a question of time before somebody else recognizes you. So how lucky can you always hope to be?"

Longarm shrugged and said, "Neither one of us would ever wear any badge if we lost all hope our luck might hold out. I learned as a schoolboy that kids who weren't ready to play for keeps had no call to play marbles after school in the first place."

Travis sighed and said, "I know. The kids who wouldn't play us for keeps grew up to be our bankers and they still want us to help them keep their marbles. Why do you reckon we try . . . ah, Mister Crawford?"

Longarm smiled wolfishly and said, "The way we get to play is more fun. When the roll is called up yonder, do you want to say you played the few marbles you had, to win, or would you rather admit you never won nor lost because you were afraid to play for keeps?"

Travis laughed, said they'd likely both die with their boots on, and they rejoined the huddle over the still form of Hernando Nana.

The local authorities had been talking as well. The town law who'd been holding Longarm's sixgun handed it back, saying, "No sense in my arresting a man for gunning a wanted outlaw in self-defense. But you don't want to leave town for a spell. You may be in for some bounty money and Doc, here, says the county may want you to bear witness at a formal inquest once he wires all this bullshit in to Fort Stockton. That's our county seat these days.''

Longarm made himself sound more reluctant than he felt as he told them he'd stick around, seeing he had no choice. It would have been dumb to tell them they'd played right into his hands by giving a man with no visible means and excuse to hang around a small town where he couldn't seem to find any job.

He had to hang about making small talk until a stretcher crew came to tote the dead man and his belongings to the meat wagon, drawn up at the edge of the graveyard. As the gathering began to break up, Longarm headed back toward the plaza, to be cut from the herd by Chongo and a couple of his crew.

It was getting easier to see why they called him Chongo. A chongo bull had it's horns on upside down, and no Spanish bullfighter wanted to mess with a chongo because you just never knew which way it meant to hook with it's contrary head. The man called Chongo said, ''We just heard you'd gunned a pal of Devil Dave Deveruex. Would you like a deal on a fast fresh pony?''

Longarm headed back to *El Paseo* with the three of them in tow as he sighed and said, ''I would if I could. They just told me not to leave town until further notice. I don't know who that was I just had to shoot. They say he was some Mission Apache living Mex. I had to shoot him because he drew on me and said mean things about my dear old mother. I don't know why. I'd never seen him before and he surely never met my mother!''

Chongo said, ''If he was the 'Pache I suspect he was he wouldn't have needed much reason. Young Dave Deveruex got Miss Connie to hire old Hernando on for a trail drive three or four summers back. She had to fire him directly for fighting with the trail cook. Don't ever fight with the cook if you want to ride for the D Bar L.''

82

"Or any other outfit," Longarm agreed, adding, "He must have had me mixed up with somebody else he'd had trouble with in the past. I never got past *Buenoches* before he slapped leather on me."

Chongo trudged in thoughtful silence for a few paces before saying, "You must draw pretty fast. Old Hernando had his faults, but a slow draw wasn't one of 'em and you did say you rode with Dick Brewer and them Regulators back in '78, didn't you?"

Longarm shook his head and said, "I did not. Miss Connie just now asked me the same questions, and, like I told her, a mere handful of soreheads feuded for all of six months and it was over before most of 'em knew it was starting to get serious. With neither Uncle John Chisum, Major Murphy, nor stockman Jim Dolan wanting anything more to do with any hired guns, the surviving gun hands all went back to working cows or riding the owlhoot trail. The newspapers barely mentioned any Billy The Kid until he escaped from that showdown and burn-out at Lawyer McSween's place in Lincoln and gunned an Indian agent called Bernstein in the process of robbing the Mescaleros. Like I keep telling everybody, nobody knows where The Kid and his few remaining pals might be this spring. Some say he's taken to robbing the Chisum herd to make up for back wages. Others have him washing dishes in a saloon near the border on the far side of El Paso. You have my word I never rode for anybody as a hired gun!"

Chongo shrugged and said, "You must have practiced some on your own to beat Hernando Nana to the draw and nail him with one shot. Were you in that *real* war, back East?"

Longarm said, "I disremember. Are you writing a book about me?"

"Just curious. Don't get your bowels in an uproar," Chongo replied in a too cheerful voice, adding, "Hernando was a heap bad Injun and no friend of me and mine if that's what you're worried about. I was only trying to figure the odds on your staying alive long enough to ride on out of here in one piece. I told you young Dave Deveruex tried to fix him up with that job and there's another bad man called Hogan you want to watch out for, too.''

Longarm said, "I'm watching. What does this Hogan look like and just where might you stand should push come to shove with Consuela Deveruex y Lopez and this younger brother I've been hearing so much about?"

Chongo soberly replied, "Me and my boys do as Miss Connie says. She don't like to be called Consuela. I don't know how she wants us to cope with her kid brother and his pals. She ain't told us yet. I only know the sidekick called Hogan by rep. They say he's mean and wild, too. Did that ranger say anything more about Greek Steve just now?"

Longarm laughed dryly and said, "I was wondering what this was all about. As a matter of fact he never mentioned any Greeks this time. He was the one who identified the man I'd shot and got me out of being arrested. They told me I was likely in the clear but ordered me to stick around."

They were back on the lantern-lit plaza by now and a pair of ugly gals left over by *El Paseo* were eyeing them all desperately as Chongo soberly told Longarm, "That was piss poor advice. Nana was an outlaw with a bounty on his head. If I was you I'd ride on and put in for the blood money from, say, San Antone. You're only going to get your fool self killed if you linger here by the Pecos."

Longarm quietly asked, "Who's more likely to kill me, Chongo? You or Miss Connie's kid brother and his pals?"

Chongo soberly replied, "Like I just told you, it's up to her."

Chapter 11

Having had his own *siesta* through the heat of day, that same Caddo kid was making up for it by sweeping in the tack room when Longarm got back to the town livery. He tipped the stable hand another nickel and explained he wanted the throw rope from the stock saddle he'd left in their keeping.

As he unbuckled the coil of oiled hemp from the swells, the young Indian leaned on his broom handle to observe, "There was another cow hand asking about that saddle and the buckskin we're boarding for you. He seemed to think you were a lawman, Mister Crawford."

Longarm held the rope coiled with his left hand as he bought time by buckling the retaining strap with his right hand and some skill left over from his earlier days west of the Big Muddy. He tried not to sound too curious as he replied, "I reckon that's better than being taken for a hired gun. Nobody seems to believe I never rode for either side in that Lincoln County War. Do you reckon that was Billy The Kid asking about me and old Buck?"

The young Caddo laughed, sort of bitter, and answered without the least hesitation, "I sort of doubt it. This one was dressed like a Mex *vaquero* and trying to talk like one. But he was as Indian as me, for all his greaser ways!"

The Texas Caddo might not have noticed he was talking

with his hands as well as his Texas-twang. A white rider less familiar with the Sign Lingo used by all the plains nations might not have noticed the way the boy seemed to brush two fingers across his own eyes as he called the other customer an Indian.

Longarm turned away from the saddle rack to smile at the stable hand uncertainly as he asked, "You say he was Apache?"

The Caddo blinked and asked, "Did I? Now that you mention it, he sure as shit wasn't Caddo. I hate it when some damned Kiowa-'Pache or Yaqui from south of the border tries to cozy up to me with that old shit about us all sticking together. It's easier to tell where I stand with *your* kind. I never asked what his nation was, once I saw he wasn't a Caddo or even a fucking Wichita. But the last I heard, the 'Pache were down in the Candelarias, south of the border."

Longarm shrugged and said, "So the Tenth Cav hopes, after that big brawl at Ojo Caliente last fall. I don't think the Indian cowboy we're talking about could be a Bronco Apache. But I do suspect he caught up with me near the church a little while ago."

The Indian kid said, "Somebody was just talking about a shoot-out in the Papist graveyard this evening. Said some Mex had been shot by the Texas Rangers. You say you were there at the time?"

To which Longarm truthfully replied, "Neither passing as a *vaquero* nor a Texas Ranger. They told *me* the sport that lost was called Nana. Hernando Nana. You're turn."

The Caddo shrugged and said, "The one I talked to never said his name nor signed his nation as he tried to get me to tell him his fortune without crossing my palm with silver. I told him I neither knew nor gave a bucket of warm spit who'd left that there saddle with us."

Longarm could take a hint. He crossed the kid's palm with another nickel and told him to keep up the good work. Then he left with the forty feet of throw-rope and circled the plaza wide, this time, lest he have to answer more pesky questions,

86

such as where was he bound and did he have a properly sworn-out search warrant.

Longarm was sworn to uphold the U.S. Constitution and inclined to treat suspects more fairly than the Bill of Rights required within the letter of the law. But on the other hand he sometimes found the *letter* bucked the *spirit* of the law, as anyone with a lick of common sense and a fair mind could see. So, what the hell, he wasn't calling on anyone in his officious capacity. He was only acting in what Billy Vail, his ownself, called the Process of Eliminating.

The street grids of Spanish-speaking towns tended to hark back to those of the ancient Romans, who'd taught the wild-men of Iberia to build towns in the first place. So the *calles* were narrow, next to Anglo streets, whilst the blocks between were bigger because of the way ancient Romans and modern Latins built their houses sort of inside out, around their yards instead of in the middle of the same, with the mostly blank outer walls smack up against the neighbor's, or sometimes the very same wall shared by two families that hardly gave toad squat about one another.

Longarm found a crooked service alley he could follow around to the rear of the Deveruex-Lopez town house, where a postern gate let folk in or out a back way.

He wasn't surprised. Fancier families didn't have back entrances just to be sneaky, albeit some might be. The posterns of old-timey Spanish castles had been kept for less romantic reasons than any siege by the Moors. You could run hired help and garbage in and out without tracking up your patio entrance and, instead of needing a servant to let company in or out, there was generally just a latch string hanging in or out and . . . what the hell?

There was just enough moonlight for Longarm to make out the white maguey braid and brass ring against the nail-studded oak of the alley postern. The string lifted the latch bar on the inside. When you aimed to shut down for the night you hauled the latch string inside, where nobody could use it from the outside. When a latch string was hanging outside, it meant company was welcome whether they knocked first or not.

Unless, of course, it was a trap. Somebody expecting an *unwelcome* guest could lay in wait or set up an infernal machine in hopes a foe might pull that inviting latch string like a fool.

So Longarm stuck to his first plan. He moved along to where he was just past their property line and shook out a noose and fifteen feet of oiled hemp.

Travel books written by folk who'd never tried to *build* anything tended to describe the Hispano-Moorish-American-Indian architecture of the Southwest as quainter than intended. Nobody had stuck all those *pueblo vigas* out through the upper surfaces of 'dobe walls like lined-up cigars for *decoration*. They were the ends of log rafters, poked on through to the outside of the thick but not-too-solid walls of glorified mud, so's the flat roofs would be more likely to stay put. But a viga could serve more than one purpose if a fair roper stood under one in the moonlight and skimmed a loop about the size of a kid's hoop in much the same way.

Longarm caught a viga with his second throw and went up the hemp hand-over-hand to roll himself over the 'dobe parapet and haul the rope up after himself whilst he gave anybody under him in the rooms below time to decided whether they'd heard something or not.

When nothing happened for what felt like a million years Longarm slowly rose, coil in hand, to ease along the edge of the flat roofing until he was over that postern gate some more. He'd just gotten there when he heard footsteps in the alley below. He hunkered down and took off his Stetson, but risked exposing the top of his skull and two eyes above the eroded 'dobe betwixt the rest of him and whoever that might be at that hour.

It looked to be the little old Widow Deveruex and a spookier figure in the habit of a Papist monk or nun. Before the two of them could get close enough for Longarm to tell, they stopped in an archway, back-lit by a street lamp beyond, and whispered at one another for a spell before the little old Mexican lady came on alone as her sort of spooky escort headed back into the mysterious night some more.

As Longarm watched, the sparrowlike older woman in black let herself in down below without disturbing any of her help, simply by pulling the latch string she'd left off for her ownself.

Thinking about that, Longarm muttered, "All right, you lit out on us, unexpected, and I bought your daughter's story you were feeling poorly. Miss Connie might have thought you'd gone to your room, too. We'll set that on the back of the stove for now."

He moved over to their rooftop water tank, knowing it's legs had to be stronger than even a thick 'dobe chimney and blessing whoever it had been downstairs who'd added modern indoor plumbing to this old mud pie.

Securing his noose around a steel valve wheel he payed out his rope inward to the patio side, uncoiling with care as he silently asked the old lady in black where she'd lit out for in such a hurry. As he judged the time, she could have left the house by way of that postern gate before or after he'd parted with her daughter, earlier than they might have expected, to catch that known associate of Devil Dave's by surprise in that churchyard. Had the plan been for the late Hernando Nana to lay for somebody coming out the patio gate down yonder?

Longarm dropped the end of the throw rope over the edge, waited to see if anybody cared, and when he saw or heard nothing from below but the soft whisper of that water fountain, he let himself over the edge with his knuckles whiter on the rope than a two story fall might call for. He wasn't worried about falling to the fig trees and ferns below. But it made one's asshole pucker when you had to expose most of your own dangling body to anyone on the top balcony before you could see if there might be anybody on the top balcony!

There wasn't. Longarm was glad, as he swung himself in over the oak railing of the second story balcony that wrapped clean around the open patio. There was a lantern shedding its soft light on that central fountain and some of the surrounding tiles and potted plants. But the balcony he found himself alone on was dark as he'd hoped for, save for a few lamp-lit windows here and there all around. So he drew his .44–40 and eased forward a few paces. Then he hunkered down to take off those noisy spurs he'd bought for show in Denver. He didn't want anybody looking at his boots at the moment. He didn't want them to mistake him for a sneaky Santa Claus checking up on good little boys and girls, either. So he stuffed the spurs in a hip pocket with the rowels in too tight to clink at all.

He moved on toward a dark but open window to hear some gal moaning, *"¡Ay, chinge me, Querido, chinge me mucho!"*

He somehow doubted either his mother or his sister would be begging Devil Dave to screw them a heap. But the place seemed to be crawling with serving gals and . . . Then the man inside was begging for mercy and another *Maria Juana que fumar* in a tone Longarm recalled as that of a snooty butler in high-toned livery, earlier. Which only went to show you couldn't tell a dope-smoking fornicator by his outfit.

All the bedrooms, as usual, were on the second floor to catch the cooler summer breezes. Those of the household help seemed to be over the stables and kitchen to either side of that postern gate below. As he got around toward the front he spied lights inside and managed to dismiss most of those rooms as empty or hardly occupied by Devil Dave and the last of his gang.

That figured to be the one they called Hogan, unless they'd picked up new members since shooting their way out of Denver. Meeting up with anybody along the owlhoot trail could be tough, since riders of the owlhoot trail by definition didn't want to meet up with anybody. So it was possible they'd beelined for Devil Dave's home range with fresh blood in mind. They wouldn't have planned on losing one quarter of the quartet before they could get out of the federal building. They'd just been reduced by a full half, over to that churchyard. So Devil Dave and his pal Hogan ought to be feeling lonesome as all get-out and . . . What might that inspire? Suspecting a stranger on a pale horse and sending old Hernando after him hadn't worked too well.

As he risked a peek around the edge of a larger lamp-lit window he saw Consuela Deveruex y Lopez and her mother sitting on a four-poster bed made up with maroon silk covers. The daughter of the house was holding the sobbing older woman in her arms, as if she was the momma and her mother was the hurt or frightened girl-child. Longarm wanted to barge on in and comfort the two of them, but he doubted that would be the way to get a lick of truth out of them and, what the hell, with any luck the old lady was dying of some female complaint instead of sheltering her wayward youth, Devil Dave.

As far as Longarm could tell, the rangers were right about his want not being hidden on the premises. That big land grant they owned made way more sense, even though the rangers did say they'd patted it down for escaped killers. A remote line-shack or, hell, an unmapped gulch or patch of bottomland swamp made more sense than the known address of his momma's town house!

Longarm worked his way back to the hanging rope and hauled himself up to stand on the railing, fixing to roll over the edge to the flat roof, let himself back down to the alley and so on. Then he had a better notion.

By standing on the balcony rail and whipping the heavy oiled hemp in a series of waves with his free hand, Longarm managed to work the noose up, then off that valve fixture up above.

Once he had, he simply recoiled his throw rope, dropped lightly to the balcony's thick planks with his sixgun back in its holster, and moved quietly but boldly down the stairs, hoping to be taken for a man who belonged there if anybody heard him at all.

Folk half asleep, tearing off some ass or reading in bed would be more likely to perk up at the sneaky sounds of somebody pussyfooting in the dark, whilst a big house staffed with a heap of help was likely to have all sorts of coming and goings through the early half of any night.

He saw he'd guessed right when he passed a lamp-lit window and the stable boy inside, mending harness at a work bench, never looked up.

There was nobody at all in the kitchen. That reminded Longarm he hadn't ever had his damned supper. But he resisted the temptation and eased past the open kitchen doorway, ignoring the smells from the banked ovens inside. You could smell Mex cooking long after they'd cleared the table and washed the dishes. But he knew, now, he wanted some beef *tamales* smothered in *chili con carne* to go with that hearty bowl of *sopa menuda*.

He found the archway leading to the rear postern gate. He was still thinking of his stomach as he almost stepped blithely into the trap set to blow his ass off.

Then, as he soberly examined the double-barreled shotgun latched to a chair with its back to one wall of the 'dobe archway, he saw it was set up to blow the nuts and guts out of anyone pulling the postern gate open from the far side. The string running from the two triggers, through an eye bolt, to that nailhead of the postern gate, had just enough slack in it to allow the intended victim to open the gate wide before the gun went off in the dark.

Longarm decided he might as well leave by the street entrance. As he eased around the dark edges of the patio he muttered, "Don't stop what you're screwing for me. I'll let my ownself out and I take back what I just said about comforting those two sad-eyed gals. Both Devil Dave's big sister and his little weepy momma seem perfectly capable of taking care of themselves!"

But as he slipped out the front gate and moved away in the night he still had no idea just who they'd planned such a nasty surprise for!

Chapter 12

Longarm holed up in his hired room for the rest of a mighty long night whilst his mind ran around in tight circles. They'd beaten him to Devil Dave's home range and whether they knew who *he* was or not they seemed to suspect something, and he seemed damned if he did and damned if he didn't drop his fool act.

Once he came out in the open with his cards on the table he'd be just another lawman looking over the shoulders of all the other lawmen who'd been searching in vain in these parts. Devil Dave and that last sidekick called Hogan would dig in deeper or light out entire. Longarm had no idea what Hogan looked like, and Devil Dave had lit out other times when they crowded him here along the Pecos.

Meanwhile he was wanted in heaps of other places and might stay close to his boyhood surroundings if he wasn't dead certain a lawman he seemed to fear more than most might was nearby. Knowing Longarm knew him on sight, he'd sent Nana to that livery with those questions.

"How come?" Longarm asked himself as he paced the tiny room in the dark, puffing a cheroot in the nude. That one Indian wouldn't have pestered that Indian stable hand at all if they'd been certain. Something or somebody had warned Devil Dave a stranger answering to a description he found ominous had ridden in, giving off mixed signals. Longarm had gone out of his way to manage that. There'd been little or nothing he could do about his overall impression without giving up more of an edge than the shits he was after deserved.

A rider could ride most any mount aboard any sensible saddle and he could only dress so many ways before he stood out more than he wanted.

The West was awash with riders who favored cross-draw or the handy combination of a sidearm and saddle gun chambered for the same common Smith & Wesson Patent .44–40–200 rounds. So he'd have been a chump to pack weapons he was less familiar with, and there was just no way a tall, tanned hombre could make himself get short and pale without serious injury to his health.

"If they're sure, they'll either run for it or come for me," he told himself as he strode through swirls of smoke in the gloom of his lonely cell-like–hired room.

If they ran they'd be long gone before he'd know they'd left. If they came for him, he knew Devil Dave on sight and those odds seemed to favor his more experienced gun hand. He had no idea how good the mysterious Hogan might be. It was hard to judge a man's chances to win or lose at anything when you had no idea what he looked like!

He blew smoke out his nostrils as he charged the open window with its view of nothing much and decided, *They'll know who they're up against or they won't. If they already know, my saying I'm me won't make no nevermind. If they're not sure about me, leaving them unsure might give me the whisker of an edge. They've both thrown down on the innocent and unaware before. But they might not draw as desperate if there's any chance I'm just some asshole they're out to kill just to stay on the safe side.*

Once he'd made up his mind about that, and seeing he'd smoked most of that cheroot down, Longarm flopped atop the rumpled sheets to see if he could catch forty winks. For it was hell to throw down and aim with sleepy eyes. But as soon as his head hit the pillow, it filled up with other puzzles to ponder because as long as he hid his true self from the local folk, he couldn't just ask questions that might have simple answers.

The old lady who'd jumped up and run out of the room around the time they'd be holding vespers, or what some Protestants called Even-song services at that nearby church, could have suddenly got religious, or she might have spoke more English than she let on and had something she'd suddenly wanted to tell somebody else.

He went over the conversation he'd had with the daughter of the house. They'd mostly talked about that Lincoln County War he hadn't ridden in and a suddenly notorious young gun waddie he might or might not have met more recent up New Mexico way on another mission entire. Longarm couldn't think of a thing he'd said about Billy The Kid that might interest Devil Dave or his dear little Mexican momma. She might have just felt tired of trying to follow a conversation in English. An old lady who'd gotten old in Texas without learning to speak English sounded like an old lady who couldn't be too interested in the world around her.

Then how come she'd been off somewhere after dark with that cowled monk, nun, or whatever? And who had they set that shotgun up to blow back out the postern gate?

Longarm didn't see how it could have been himself, no matter how two-faced anybody was. Both Devil Dave's big sister and little mother had him set up inside the house, figuring to leave by the front gate, at the time the older one had scuttled off on her mysterious errand.

That shotgun trap couldn't have been set up to kill *her* because it hadn't. He'd been watching as she'd opened the postern gate and gone on inside. Had she been worried about somebody following her?

Or had it simply been customary burglar insurance, followed every night as they locked themselves in against all comers? Most American states had laws against such notions, but Longarm knew that back in some old countries it was lawful to set up man traps designed to kill or maim. A Lime Juicer riding for the Thompson brothers had once told Longarm about this English lord who'd set up dozens of powerful bear traps to catch kids poaching rabbits on his big, old, private woodlot.

Spanish grandees had been known to have wandering gypsies shot on sight as trespassers whether they were acting suspicious or not. So it might be best to set that shotgun trap aside until somebody walked into it, and, as for that gun slinger popping out of the neighborhood church just after those evening vespers . . . The old lady wouldn't have been allowed to stay after they were locking up, and had she hidden in some nook, as that Mission Apache might have, nobody from said church would have been escorting her home, unless . . .

"We're going to have to do some confessing to that priest and hope he's good at keeping secrets!" Longarm muttered aloud.

Back in Denver, Miss Morgana Floyd of the Arvada Orphan Asylum and that swamping cathedral on Capitol Hill had told him she went every Saturday to tell her father confessor about the fresh ways he'd been treating her, and so far she'd been given a tedious number of "Hail Mary's" to recite, but not a word about her liking it with the lamps lit had appeared in the *Rocky Mountain News*. Few Protestants or Jews got to confess their sins and be forgiven before they could die and settle up with a higher authority.

Longarm knew, as a lawman, that many a Mex bandit or Mission Indian had cheerfully confessed to murder, rape, and worse without getting turned in by their priests. But could a West-by-God-Virginia boy who'd dropped out of Sunday school early ask for the same deal? And what was that stuff about the same church offering Sanctuary to outlaws on the run?

Longarm read more than he liked to let on. Reading alone in bed near the end of the month before payday had just being alone beat by a country mile. So he'd read that yarn by Mister Victor Hugo about a big swamping church in Paris, France, where the hunchbacked bell ringer had given sanctuary to a gypsy gal wanted by the law. So what if, all this time, Devil Dave and his pals had been hiding out in the belfry of that church near the family town house?

That priest had said he hadn't known the late Hernando Nana and had no idea what he'd been doing in the hallway, at least, of the rectory. Longarm had heard or read somewhere else that such men of the cloth were allowed to keep secrets from the law but not to *lie* outright to anybody.

Longarm wasn't supposed to tell fibs in the line of duty, either. Meanwhile, a church in the Mex barrio where rangers seldom prayed made a swell place to meet one's momma when she had some money or information for you, whether you were sleeping on the premises or somewheres else the rest of the time.

He decided he'd just have to risk a man-to-man talk with that boss priest come morning, and having made up his mind, he was soon in another bed—a four-poster—with the ready and willing Consuela Deveruex y Lopez, but for some damned reason, unable to get it in her tight little ring-dang-doo whilst she pleaded with him to *chingate*, which meant "Go fuck yourself" as soon as you studied on it, and made no sense in the context she kept saying it, whilst he tried in vain to fuck *her*. So he decided none of it made much sense and having seen he was in an impossible situation, woke up.

He was glad that had all been a dream. Billy Vail would have had a fit if he'd really gotten it in Devil Dave's sister. Yet it did seem a shame how you could only seem to get so far and never all the way in one of those so-called wet dreams. You probably had to be a determined celibate who never jerked off to have an all-out really wet dream. But a man who dreamed anything sassy about a possible arrest had a dirty mind he'd best keep an eye on.

The sun was not only up but lancing through the one-slit window of his dinky cell. So Longarm washed up at the corner dry-sink with the brown soap, string rag, and *olla* of water provided. But he skipped a fresh shave with cold water lest somebody take him for respectable and put his trail-dusted jeans, shirt, and bolero jacket on over the clean underwear he'd snuck from a saddle bag.

He put those flashy spurs back on his scuffed boots over clean socks nobody could see. He'd naturally cleaned his three guns before turning in the night before. He field stripped and wiped down all the parts of his sixgun, derringer, and saddle gun with a fresh patch, lightly oiled, because once upon a time a wise old ordinance sergeant had told young Private Long that you just never got to maintain a gun worth mention in the middle of a gunfight, and a well-tended Springfield .52 rifled musket had saved his ass at Shiloh by going off just when his trigger finger had wanted it to, during an enemy trooper's hang-fire.

He left the fifteen shot .44–40 Winchester '73 on the bed as he went to breakfast with his sixgun on his left hip and his double derringer in an inside pocket of his jacket, across from his cheroots and watch, with the usual gold-washed chain hidden away with his shoestring tie and other such notions.

He had his fried eggs over a T-bone, with plenty of Tex-Mex black coffee and a slab of tuna pie for breakfast. He always ordered tuna pie when he was close to the border. Up Denver way they tended to look at you funny when you asked if they served tuna pie. They seemed to think you were ordering a pie made out of fish instead of the sweet red tuna fruits off cactus hedges.

As he was washing the last of his tuna pie down, Ranger Travis came in off the street to declare, "I was hoping I'd run across you before we rode out. I don't reckon we could interest you in scouting Indians for us, eh?"

Longarm shoved his plate away and reached for a smoke as he soberly replied, "Not hardly. I told you Judge Dickerson of the Denver District Court wants Devil Dave Deveruex dead or alive. Hogan sounds like a sort of Irish name and

Hogan's the last of them three who busted the kid out of Judge Dickerson's courtroom. He might be a breed. I take it you ain't talking about hunting breeds, just now?"

The Texas Ranger shook his head and said, "Victorio, with up to a hundred Bronco Apache who've joined him in the Candelarias. The Mexican *federales* are working with Texas and the U.S. Army for a change. So we have that ornery Apache bouncing around like spit on a hot stove and a hundred Texas Rangers have been detailed to scout for the Ninth Cav. Ain't that a bitch?"

Longarm shrugged and said, "The Ninth and Tenth are both good outfits to fight alongside, despite or perhaps because of their complexions I know some former Union officers refuse to lead colored troops. But a heap of ex-slaves seem anxious to prove themselves, and none of those colored regiments have the desertion rate of some whiter ones."

The Texican snorted, "Hell, I ain't worried about riding against old Victorio with colored boys who've fit *Comanche* and won. I just don't cotton to the notion of leaving you here on your own. If I was you I'd at least level with the town marshal and have him covering my back."

Longarm offered a cheroot to the ranger and stuck the other betwixt his own teeth as he said, "You ain't me. I wouldn't have told you who I was or what I was doing here if you hadn't already known. It ain't that I distrust all other lawmen. I've just found it troubles my mind less to worry about myself alone as I wander down dark alleyways, and nobody can betray any secrets you just don't tell them. I've already got more balls in the air than my head can juggle sensible."

He brought the ranger up to date on his adventures since they'd spoken the night before. Travis allowed that Mexicans often rigged up the hen-house door with a shotgun trap and seemed to feel it cut down on chicken stealing. He said they'd already figured the old widow woman was what his Irish kin called a "Shawlee" or one of those sad little women you saw haunting Papist churches betwixt services, mumbling their rosaries sort of mindless, touched in the head or perhaps just lonesome and afraid.

Longarm said he hadn't known what sort of name Travis might be.

The Texican said, "Travis is the Lancashire spelling of gatekeeper man. My English granther traveled to Texas where he rescued a young lady of the Hebrew persuasion from the Comanche. She was pretty, even in old age, and being the same Comanche had killed the gent of her own faith who'd sent east for her, they got hitched, and so, according to Torah, my daddy, having a Jewish momma, was a Jew named Travis who prayed Episcopalian 'til he married my Irish-Mex momma, who tried to raise us in her two varieties of The True Faith. The most educational part for me was the way the different branches of my family mean-mouthed one another's religions without knowing all that much about any. You might say it left me with an open mind."

Longarm said, "I've been looking for somebody like you to tell me how much I might be able to trust that priest we met up with last night. Would he be honor-bound to keep it under his hat if I told him who I was, and do you know how Rome feels about that Sanctuary stuff?"

The Protestant, Jewish, Catholic ranger shrugged and said, "I reckon nine out of ten priests respect secrets confided to them alone. As for the granting of Sanctuary, they ain't supposed to shelter common felons, and they're supposed to inform the local authorities they've given the Sanctuary of the Church to a want, no matter what he or she might be wanted for."

Longarm insisted, "Are you saying no priest would hide Devil Dave or his pals without telling us he was doing so?"

The ranger who claimed to know shook his head and said, "What Rome says and what a particular man of the cloth might do ain't the same tidy package at all. Like I said, you may be able to trust your life to *most* such sky pilots. But Our Lord only had to trust *His* life to that one bad apple out of a dozen to end up in a mighty mean situation!"

100

Chapter 13

You had to play such chips as you had left with the cards you were dealt, unless you aimed to just get up and leave the table, safe and dumb. Longarm hadn't found anyone in Texas who was willing to own up to the whereabouts of Devil Dave and the less distinct Hogan, wanted on that same murder warrant after shooting up that Denver courtroom.

When he got over to the rectory that same old priest seemed to have been expecting him. He ushered Longarm into a Spartan study, sat him in a comfortable leather chair, and rang for refreshments as he helped his ownself to a straight-back seat left over from the Spanish Inquisition and said, "I have wondered when you would get around to us, *El Brazo Largo.*"

Longarm started to deny it. Then he smiled sheepishly and allowed, "That's what comes of having every Spanish speaker in town attending the same church, I reckon."

The older man sighed and said, "If only. Let us be frank with one another, Deputy Long. The late Benito Juarez was of pure Indian blood and had little use for a church he felt had repressed his own Zapotec ancestors. Perhaps it had. I know little of the religious practices of the Zapotec. When Cortez entered *Ciudad Mejico* he had an army of Indian rebels following him and his few Spanish men-at-arms. The Aztecs

101

your Yanqui schoolbooks feel so sorry for had terrorized the country coast-to-coast with their demands for slaves and human sacrifices. Our Mother Church put an end to this. Aztec priests wearing human bones and painted with human blood were executed as murderers by the new Spanish rulers, and you may have heard how complex a man we had in our own Archbishop Juan De Fonesca, no?''

Longarm said, ''No. I ain't never seen a warrant sworn out against a gent by that name, Padre.''

The priest smiled thinly and replied, ''Perhaps that is because he died some time ago. Ferdinand and Isabella authorized him to look after their new subjects in New Spain. De Fonesca spoke up for the Indians and had laws passed for to protect them from being exploited. He also burned many Aztec books and a good many Aztec priests. To protect the Indians from forced labor he authorized each Spanish family to import up to twelve Africans who were already slaves. As you may have guessed, that did not work out exactly as planned. Thousands of Africans who had not been slaves until then were rounded up and transported to the New World while the Indians were exploited just the same.''

Longarm asked, ''Why are you telling me all this, Padre? I'm having enough trouble understanding Mexico in the here and now!''

A Mex gal in a maid's uniform brought a tray in, piled with pastries, a pitcher of sangria, and cut glass goblets. As she served the two of them the Mexican priest said, ''The Mexico of today is left over from the Mexico of yesterday, so close to *Los Estados Unidos*, so far from God, with so many mistakes by well-meaning fools and deep-dyed sinners still haunting her and her people.''

He indicated that Longarm was to dig in as he continued. ''Is impossible for most Mexicans to really understand the mess we call Mexico. I only wish for you to understand my own position a little. Was a priest by the name of Hidalgo who first led an uprising for Mexico's liberty in 1811. They killed him, of course, and took unjust revenge on the rest of us, as the winners always do. So those churchmen who survived tried for to, how you say, patch things up with the Spanish ruling class and, perhaps, some went a little too far.''

Longarm sipped some sangria, noting this batch had been mixed with finer wine, and allowed he'd heard Juarez had confiscated a heap of church property once his working-class party got to running things.

His host sighed, ''Then that fool, Napoleon the Second, sent an even bigger fool called Maximilian in with the French Foreign Legion to put things back the way they'd been, and the next time Juarez won he was *really* mad! The persecution of priests, monks, and nuns that followed was an ugly chapter our current liberals do not wish for to talk about. When Juarez died, one of his generals, Porfirio Diaz, took over in perhaps an irregular manner.''

Longarm growled, ''You mean he stole *La Revolucián*, the ruthless son of a bitch!''

The old priest nodded in agreement but demurred, ''A ruthless *smart* son of a bitch who does not like surprises. He has made friends up in Washington and along your Wall Street by restoring law and order in a country sadly lacking either. His position with regard to the Church of Rome has been, how you say, a compromise. He and his strongarms in gray sombreros leave us alone and we, in turn, leave them alone. My official position, as far as a known enemy of the Diaz Government is concerned, is that I have no wish to aid or abet this *Yanqui* wildman called *El Brazo Largo* by so many of my poor misguided people.''

Longarm set his half-drained goblet aside and started to rise as he thanked the old cuss for what he'd already swallowed.

The priest said, ''*Sentarse*, I had not finished. In my capacity as a priest of *La Santa Fe* I would have nothing for to say to this most *desicreditado* enemy of El Presidente Diaz. So perhaps it is just as well I have only heard rumors he might be in town and for how may I help you in your capacity as a lawman on *this* side of the border?''

Longarm chose his words before he cautiously replied, "To start with, was it the Widow Deveruex or her daughter who told you who I . . . might be, Padre?"

The priest said, "I do not think they know who you are. I can tell you that much. I am not at liberty to discuss what anyone may or may not have told me in the confessional. Now you wish for me to tell you whether poor David Deveruex or his comrades have sought Sanctuary with us, no?"

Longarm nodded and said, "Yep. Ain't a question I can come up with more important than that one, Padre."

The older man sighed and said, "You have my word as an ordained man of God that David and his friend, Hogan, are nowhere to be found on the property of this parish, including some grazing land you will hear of as you ask around."

Longarm sipped more sangria and asked, "Is it safe to say you'd tell me if he was somewhere else you knew of, Padre?"

The priest looked pained and replied, "Let us not play guessing games, my son. I have tried for to explain the delicate position I am in with some of my parish on one side while others stand ready to fight to the death for the other. I have told you as much as I have because I do not wish for you to make more trouble for anyone. The ones you seek are not here. They are not hiding with anyone who attends services at this church. That is all I can tell you. Please do not ask me to betray a confidence or lie to a lawman of these *Estados Unidos*!"

So Longarm never. It would have been dumb to brag to the older man he'd used that "process of eliminating" to put the murderous little pissant out on the Deveruex–Lopez Grant, with his big sister instead of his little old momma covering up for him!

He finished the sangria and one of the *galetta dulces* to be polite and left the rectory friendly without pressing the priest about Hernando Nana popping out this same door like that the night before. The friendly old cuss had already told him more than he'd hoped for. So all he had to do now was search for an armed-and-dangerous needle in one hellishly big mesquite stack! That son of a bitching land grant covered many a square mile of rough range and it hardly seemed likely any D Bar L riders would be offering a helping hand to anybody but the bratty kid brother of their boss lady, Devil Dave's own sister!

Springtime in West Texas was hot as High Summer in Denver. So Longarm paused in the shade of a blackjack arching over the churchyard walk to light a fresh cheroot as he tried to come up with some way to poke about the D Bar L without being challenged as a trespasser by riders who'd know their own range better.

As he shook out the match a ragged-ass Mexican kid came through the tombstones like a haunt fixing to ask for a hand-out. Longarm had made the mistake of giving money to one kid begging in Spanish. So he said, *"No me jodas, Muchacho. No tengo dinero. No tengo tabaco. No tengo mierda por Usted. ¿Comprende?"*

To which the kid sweetly replied. *"Chingate!* I do not wish for your money. I do not wish for tobacco and you can keep your shit! I was told you are the gringo called Dunk Crawford. The *viada* who sent me for to find you and bring you to her does not speak to me so *rudo.* But she must be *loco en las cabeza* to wish for your *visita desagradable."*

Longarm broke out another cheroot and soothed, "Have a smoke, you sassy little cuss. A widow woman sent you to fetch me, you say? Might we be talking about a little gray-haired *viada* of *calidad?"*

The kid took the cheroot without even a nod of thanks and told Longarm to judge the lady for himself. So Longarm fell in step with the kid, who put the cheroot away for later as Longarm tried to figure out where they were going.

When he asked if the Deveruex-Lopez town house wasn't more to the north of the churchyard the Mex kid snorted that everyone knew that.

So the old widow woman didn't want to meet him at home,

and like the old church song suggested, farther along he'd understand why.

As they left the churchyard Longarm asked the kid whether he went to church back yonder and the kid snorted, "*Por que?* Life is too short for to waste any part of it praying for to live forever. Do *you* believe any of that *mierda*, Señor Crawford?"

Longarm shrugged and said, "I ain't as old and sure of myself as you, *muchacho*. The reason I asked was I was wondering whether there was a convent or a monastery attached to that old Spanish church."

The kid shook his head and said, "*Ningundo de los dos.* Is a school for *muchachas* run by only a few, how you say, teaching nuns. But they take no direct orders from Padre Luis, so he is forced for to sleep with his housekeeper. For why do you ask?"

Longarm tried to sound less interested than he was when he replied he'd thought he'd seen a monk or nun walking home the widow he worked for.

The kid seemed to find this tough to buy and suggested Longarm was in the market for some specs. Longarm chose not to press the matter.

The raggedy kid led him to a part of town where the houses, albeit built of 'dobe, were set back a piece with their yards wrapped around them, Anglo style. The kid pointed ahead to a bay window bigger than any Mex would have in an outside wall, where a sign hung, advising one and all that Madame Irene made dresses to measure inside.

Longarm figured the widow woman who'd sent for him would tell him why she'd wanted to meet him in a dressmaker's shop once he asked her, if that was exactly what she, or somebody else, really had in mind.

He stopped in the shade of a blackjack oak across the way to fish in his pocket for a nickel as he told the kid he'd take it from there.

The fresh-mouthed street urchin accepted the coin without

thanking Longarm and lit out on his bare feet to wherever raggedy kids lit out to with a whole nickel.

Longarm didn't waste time wondering how a kid so young could have gotten so old and bitter. He couldn't spot anybody watching for him inside that big bay window. That didn't mean nobody could be. It only meant he had a chance. So he strode off as if he was headed somewhere else entire and didn't cross the dusty road until nary a chink in the 'dobe walls of that dressmaker's was aimed his way.

Once he made it that far it was duck-soup-simple to work around to the back alley and, sure enough, there was a back door and no yard dog when he found his way to the cactus-hedged back garden of the odd address the Widow Deveruex had given for their get-together.

Hoping he was only about to embarrass his fool self, Longarm drew his .44–40 and dashed across the sunny garden to the back door, to find it locked in his fool face.

He shifted his sixgun to his left hand and got out a pocket knife with one blade filed in a manner to get anyone but a lawman arrested. But as he silently slipped his skeleton key in the lock, the door was flung wide and a marble goddess wearing an ecru silk kimono was asking him what had kept him so long and how come he'd come pussyfooting to her kitchen door.

On second glance the statuesque figure was that of a fair-sized gal with ivory-white skin, blue-black hair pinned up in a bun, and eyes as dark and smouldering as a pissed-off Apache.

Her kimono was almost as wide open as her kitchen door and he saw she was brunette all over as he ticked his hat brim to her and allowed he'd found her invite just a tad mysterious.

She said, "Come on in before the neighbors have us going at it out in the garden. I'm Irene Pantages. Didn't that boy I sent for you tell you that?"

As he followed her inside a not unpleasant but odd-smelling kitchen Longarm replied, "He described you as a widow woman, Miss Irene. I had another lady entire in mind and that's why I thought I'd best scout an address that took me by surprise. You say you're last name would be Pantages, ma'am? The same as that of this wrangler I know?"

"By marriage," the big brunette explained, leading Longarm on through her kitchen instead of sitting him down for coffee and cake as custom called for. As he followed, admiring the view, she explained, "My late husband was the cousin of the poor relation you call Greek Steve. We Hellenes do stick together, and poor Stavros and his problems with the law are why I sent for you."

He'd expected to wind up in a front parlor if she didn't mean to coffee and cake him in her kitchen. So he was mighty surprised when they wound up in what surely seemed a lady's bed chamber, complete with a four-poster and an end table piled with smokes, tumblers, and a fifth of bourbon.

He gulped and said, "I didn't know your kinsman was in trouble with the law, Miss Irene."

She shrugged off her kimono to turn and face him bare as a babe, but ten times as tempting, as she demurely replied, "Bullshit. I know for a fact you were seen talking with a Texas Ranger before Stavros came to me for help. I know for a fact you were seen talking to that same Texas Ranger just after Stavros left town. What are you, a bounty hunter or some other sort of lawman in disguise?"

Longarm tried not to stare lower than her firm jawline as he told her she could have his word he wasn't a Texas Ranger.

She lay back on her elbows to part her ivory thighs invitingly as she decided, "You're not bad looking, whatever you are, and they tell me lawmen just hate to arrest girls they've made love to. So what are you waiting for? Don't you want to compare notes with me on Stavros?"

Longarm soberly replied, "I ain't sure. What have you got on Greek Steve, Miss Irene?"

She shook her head and insisted, "First we fuck and then we can talk."

Chapter 14

It sure beat all how women passed such helpful hints about menfolk around. And some were as dumb as the notions poolroom kids told one one another about women. But the taxpayers had the right to expect a senior deputy to do his duty, no matter how painful. So he put his hat and gun aside and got out of his boots and duds as fast as he was able, with the curvaceous creamy brunette helping him off with his underpants at the last, and grabbing hold of his old organ grinder with a wicked grin as she shoved him flat beside her marvelled, "Good heavens! Is all this meant for little old me!"

He assured her it was and rolled the other way to plant his socks on the rug and hover above her, stiff elbowed, whilst she guided it in for their mutual enjoyment.

From the way she bit her lush lower lip and thrust her generously proportioned pelvis up to meet his, he suspected she might be combining business with pleasure.

He knew *he* was. So this hardly seemed the time to say that though his boss frowned on the practice and defense lawyers delighted in a lawman getting this familiar with a client before he arrested her, it wasn't as impossible to arrest a lady you'd played slap-and-tickle with as a heap of shemale suspects had been told, Lord love whoever might have told *this* one! For she was a big strong gal with a heap of spring in her ass and a twat tight enough to service a schoolboy!

So a grand time was had by all and Longarm almost forgot the palmed derringer he'd brought to bed with them until he had to move it again when she begged him to put a second pillow under her frisky pale ass.

She felt it when he came in her, and wrapped her long ivory limbs around his waist to hold him inside her as they both went limp and he kissed her, sincere.

When they came up for air she murmured, "Oh, thank you, Dunk. I'd almost forgotten how good that could feel, with the right man."

He ground his pubic bone against her own without answering as he digested her use of his made-up name. Any D Bar L rider who'd told her he'd been messing with the rangers could have told her he was a saddle tramp they called Dunk Crawford. If she was buying the name it likely meant nobody had told her he was *El Brazo Largo*. Nobody'd said either one of them were Mexican. She and Greek Steve both talked as natural as any other West Texas folk. Greek Steve had said he'd been born and raised nearby. He decided to let her tell him about herself in her own way in her own good time.

She did as they reluctantly untangled for a drink, a smoke, and their second wind. She made sure he was comfortable with those pillows piled behind his bare shoulders, a drink in his free hand, a good cigar in his mouth, and a big creamy tit in his other hand before she took a deep breath and said, "My late husband left me well provided for with this business in town and some Mexicans herding sheep for me over on the Stockton Plateau. So from time to time I've been able to help poor Stavros a little. He needs a little help because he drinks a lot."

When a lady told a gent with a tumbler of whiskey in his hand that another gent drank a lot it was safe to say he had a problem. Longarm was suddenly reminded he had both hands occupied with his derringer under the pillow. So he gripped the Havana Claro in his teeth and put the glass aside to thoughtfully roll a nipple betwixt thumb and forefinger as

110

he soberly asked Irene if she ever helped Cousin Stavros out this way.

She gasped, "*Eutheo*! He is *family*! By marriage at any rate. And one of the reasons his money never lasts until payday is that he spends the little he doesn't spend on liquor at a bordello by the river called Rosalinda's!"

Longarm was inclined to believe her. He'd been to Rosalinda's with Greek Steve and nobody getting what Irene had to offer would spend a day's pay on any whore! Old Irene was as good a lay with twice the class of pretty little Perfidia, and that was saying something indeed.

Longarm took a drag on the Claro, put it aside in a bed-table ashtray, and finished off that whiskey before he suggested mildly, "You said there was something you wanted to talk about, once we'd gotten to know one another this well."

She snuggled closer and said, "I closed early and it's almost the usual siesta time. You've no idea how *well* I mean to know you, in the biblical sense, and Stavros was what I wanted to talk to you about."

He shrugged a bare shoulder under her soft cheek and said, "Once you say a man has a drinking problem you've said about all there could be to say about him, right?"

She toyed with the hairs on Longarm's belly as she sighed, "Wrong. He came to me last night for a loan. That's what Stavros calls it when he asks me for money, a loan. He said he needed at least twenty-five dollars. I told him that was a lot of money. He said he needed it to ride far and fast. He said the rangers had been asking you about him."

"That's what I told Chongo," Longarm cautiously admitted. That was the plain truth when you studied on it. He thought it safe to add, "I never told Chongo the rangers had accused old Steve of anything. All I told Chongo was that they'd asked if I knew a rider who made that Sign of the Cross backwards, Greek Style."

The Greek gal in bed with him sniffed and said she'd be the judge of who made the Sign of The Cross the wrong way. She added, "The rest of you have Easter on the wrong day,

111

too, but getting back to Cousin Stavros. He confessed to me that the rangers might be after him because of young David Deveruex, the kid brother of the lady he rides for. The boy's in some sort of trouble. Serious trouble. Stavros said both the rangers and some famous federal lawman are after him and some Irishman.''

Longarm asked, ''Are you sure he said the Deveruex boy was riding with an Irishman? I think I heard them rangers say something about an outlaw called Hogan, and I'll allow that sounds like an Irish name, but so does Deveruex and I understand they're half-Mex.''

The Greek-American widow woman said, ''Stavros said he hadn't met this wanted man called Hogan. But he seemed to feel he was as dangerous as David Deveruex and we all know him as Devil Dave.''

''I've heard tell he grew up mean in these parts,'' said Longarm.

The local gal suppressed a shudder and said, ''Crazy-mean. Used to rope outhouses when ladies were using them and it wasn't Halloween. Shot a black trooper in the back one Saturday evening because he declared Our Lord made darkies to fetch and carry, not to be carried around by a superior animal.''

''I heard Devil Dave was like that,'' Longarm murmured, adding, ''How does Cousin Steve tie in with such a sweet kid?''

She confessed, ''I don't know. He wouldn't tell me. I was hoping you could tell me, once I'd heard the rangers had lit out after him a few minutes after one of them had another conversation with you this morning.''

Longarm felt on surer ground as he assured her, truthfully, ''The one ranger I spoke to at breakfast time never said they were riding out after old Steve or any other white man. He said Victorio and as many as a hundred Bronco Apache have been raiding too close to Texas for comfort. He asked if I was a war vet who might like to ride along as they scout for the Ninth Cav. When did Steve light out last night? Was it early or late and did he say which way he meant to ride?''

She reached down to fondle his limp shaft as she calmly replied, ''I think I'd better compromise you as an arresting officer some more before I say another word about my criminal associates.''

Longarm laughed and asked her who'd told her he was a lawman out to arrest her or anyone in her family. But she just kept stroking it with the skill only a gal who'd been happily married a spell seemed to attain, as many a schoolboy playing stinkfinger in a porch swing had been know to complain. So, seeing it was getting so hard, and not wanting to get her soft palm messy, he set everything but her aside to roll back in the saddle again. But then she said she wanted to get on top. So he let her, and she did that as only a gal who'd had a heap of practice could hope to manage.

Smiling down at him through the soft daylight of her bedroom as she slid up and down his merry-go-round pole Irene asked him why he had his eyes shut. ''Don't you like to watch my nipples bounce?'' she demanded.

He opened his eyes with a dreamy smile to agree she bounced great, all over, and explained, ''I was just now thinking about another widow gal and a conversation we once had about the advantages of doing this with one.''

''Oh?'' she replied with a dark brow arched, ''Are you suggesting women in my position should be grateful to men for taking pity on our poor lonely twats?''

''Call it a ring-dang-doo,'' he soothed. ''Twat is a sort of ugly word for such a wonder of nature. I never meant to imply you widow women were more hard-up than say a romantic schoolmarm playing with herself alone in bed. Any bridegroom can tell you a virgin-pure can be a pain in the neck when it comes to slap-and-tickle. It takes practice before anybody gets this right!''

She gyrated her pelvis teasingly as she replied, ''Don't I know it! A girl in my position has to be very careful lest she risk her reputation with a handsome lout who comes too soon, or can't get it up at all. You're saying you prefer an experienced slut who's had plenty of practice, eh?''

To which he gallantly replied, ''Not hardly. The gals down at that whorehouse you just mentioned have doubtless had more practice than the average happy housewife could abide. But when a man has a romantic nature he feels sort of low-down dumb with a business woman who might not even like him. I know they say money can't buy love, but I'll be switched if I'll pay for *hostility*!''

The once-married Irene bit down skillfully with her innards to ask if that felt friendly enough.

He thrust upwards and replied, ''It surely do and the best part about doing this with a married woman who ain't married no more is that nobody is likely to gun you for rutting with their wife whilst, at the same time, you're getting the sort of screwing men kill one another over!''

She laughed like hell and allowed she'd take that as a compliment, if he'd roll her over and finish right.

He was willing, and Irene's notion of a good finishing position was a contortion that could have gotten her a job with P. T. Barnum, had she been able to cross her legs behind her own head like that with a modest costume on. It would have gotten the show raided had she been wearing *jeans* in that position.

But it sure felt swell, and Irene whipped up some sandwiches and had already iced some coffee to wash them down with as they whiled away one of the nicest *siestas* Longarm could recall.

When the weren't satisfying their healthy appetites at both ends they took turns trying to pry information out of one another. Longarm found it easy to jaw with the well-endowed young widow as they fondled one another, because his conscience was clear as far as Greek Steve went. He didn't have a thing on the panic-stricken wrangler and the rangers had less, seeing he'd made up all that bull about anyone suspecting Pantages of something vague.

He felt safe asking questions. Irene kept saying she'd been

114

hoping he'd know the answers to the same questions. All that was certain, if she was on the level, was that Greek Steve had darkened her door in a flap with liquor on his breath to plead for her help in getting him clean out of the valley. She said he hadn't been making much sense in either English or the half-remembered Greek he'd lapsed into when he'd told her he'd already done a bad thing and that now they were pressing him to kill somebody with the Texas Rangers reading over his shoulder.

Longarm said, "I think it was one of them rangers who said Devil Dave Deveruex is running low on sidekicks. I had a time convincing 'em I'd never seen that one Mex who must have mistook me for someone else in that churchyard last night. But why would Devil Dave want to recruit a remuda hand off his family spread as a killer? I understood old Steve was born and raised in these parts without any wants posted on his hide. You just now told me he was a sort of shiftless cuss living from one payday to the next. Yet you say Steve confessed he'd already committed one crime and they were pressing him to do worse?"

She tried to cool her bare tits with a folding Spanish fan as she told him, "Poor Stavros has no other trade to save him from the dollar a day he's worth to the D Bar L. In town he'd like it known he rides as a top hand. But he's never been able to get the knack of roping, and they have him wrangling the riding stock for Mexican kids who can rope and throw."

Longarm said, "Mexican Indians invented the roping the mixed-blood *vaquero's* so famous for. Somebody riding with Cortez wrote he'd seen an Aztec rope a running deer with his braided leather lasso. You're right about it being a knack, like pitching a baseball or playing a musical saw. Some are born with such abilities, some can learn 'em, and others are just better off trying something else."

He sat up to reach for his Stetson and fan his own bare hide some, as it kept getting warmer. She laughed and said they'd sure look silly to anybody walking in on them at the moment.

115

He said, "You told me the door was locked. We were talking about how come anyone might take Cousin Steve for a cuss who'd be willing or even able to kill another."

She replied, "I told you he drinks too much and brags too much for a poor soul who's never amounted to much. Stavros and me are both a bit older than Devil Dave Deveruex. I remember his big sister, that stuck-up dishwater blonde greaser, as about my age. We went to different schools. They're Church of Rome."

"What does that have to do with her kid brother or Cousin Steve?" he demanded.

She said, "They would not have played together as mean little kids. So they only know one another by local repute. From all accounts, Devil Dave deserves his reputation. Poor Stavros, I fear, has blown his own trumpet too loudly, trying to convince the girls at Rosalinda's that since he can't rope they must have him on the payroll as a gun hand."

Longarm nodded soberly and said, "Like that boy who cried wolf in that yarn by Mister Aesop!"

She smiled roguishly and said, "I didn't know you were that familiar with Greek culture. It feels like rain. I hope it does. If ever things cool off in here again I've some other Greek notions to teach you."

Chapter 15

It never rained that afternoon, but by sundown the dry heat outside was bearable—once they'd shared a cool tub together and proven soap could be a lot of fun, too.

He wound up on the streets of Sheffield-Crossing, alone, because she had to open her shop for the evening trade, after extending him an open invite to help her close it, around midnight.

Longarm took advantage of the tricky light to run a few errands. He was coming out of the Western Union when Chongo Masters and another gent in a more *charro* outfit, with more Indian blood in him, stopped him on the walk.

Chongo said, "Crawford, this would be Slim Gonzales, the ramrod of the D Bar L, and he's got some questions for you. So answer 'em polite."

"I've nothing to hide," Longarm lied, adding, "but after that I don't have to be polite to anybody I ain't working for, *comprende?*"

Despite his name and appearance, Gonzales had no accent as he soberly said, "Don't get your bowels in an uproar. They told me you were a big brave boy when that Mission Apache started up with you last night. I'm not looking to rawhide anybody, Dunk Crawford. I'm looking for a hand who seems to have strayed or been stolen on us."

Longarm nodded and said, "I was just talking to his cousin about him. She thought I might know where he was. I told her I hadn't noticed he was missing. You may find this hard to buy, but they don't pay this child to ride herd on the hired hands where I've never worked."

The *Tejano*, or Tex-Mex, foreman said, "You were talking to the rangers about him, and Chongo, here, tells me Greek Steve seemed mighty upset about that."

Longarm nodded and said, "Chongo told you true as far as Greek Steve went. I never told him the rangers had asked about him in particular. I told they'd asked if I knew any Greek riders in these parts and I told they I didn't know *any* riders in these parts."

Gonzales nodded but demanded, "How come Steve hasn't been seen since early last night and the rangers lit out this morning after talking to you some more?"

Longarm shrugged and replied in an easy tone, "Ask 'em. They told me they'd been called back to their posts to mount another expedition with the Buffalo Soldiers. Our army and two thousand *federales* have been out to corner Victorio and his hundred-odd Bronco Apache since last summer. I told 'em I'd been invited to a war one time and hadn't enjoyed it as much as I'd hoped I might. They never asked if I thought Greek Steve might care to ride with them against Victorio."

Chongo asked, "What were you just doing in that telegraph office?"

Longarm snorted in disgust and said, "Sending telegrams, of course. I asked if I could get a blow job off Western Union, but they said they only handled messages."

"Who did you wire?" Chongo demanded in a mighty rude tone.

Longarm said, "President Rutherford B. Hayes and the Pope in Rome. I want them to abandon the gold standard and declare me a saint. Go on and ask inside if you don't believe me!"

They must not have believed him. Slim Gonzales said, "Western Union won't show us what you just wired unless you give your permit. Let's go back inside so's you can give your permit, Dunk.''

Longarm went back inside between them, having little other choice, and the three of them bellied up to the counter, where Longarm asked the bemused gray telegraph clerk if he could have those blanks back for just a minute.

The clerk allowed it made no nevermind to him and the last two wires they'd sent were naturally on top of the out pile. So he handed them to Longarm, who handed them to Slim Gonzales, dryly asking, ''You can read plain English, I hope?''

The lanky *Tejano* could. Longarm had addressed one coded field report to the home address of old Henry, the young squirt who typed out front for Marshal Billy Vail at the Denver federal building. With just such an emergency in mind, Longarm had wired the Jingle Bob at South Spring, New Mexico Territory, asking Uncle John Chisum if he could have his old job back at the same pay, seeing the grass hadn't turned out green as he'd hoped down this way.

He'd signed it Dunk Crawford, knowing anyone who might intercept it wouldn't be anyone he'd want to show his badge and I.D. off to. It was a safer ploy than dragging no red herrings at all across a false trail. He'd known when he'd sent it that Uncle John Chisum would have no idea who Dunk Crawford might be, or whether he'd ever ridden for the Jingle Bob or not. When a reasonably polite cattle baron had hired and fired hundreds of riders in his time he'd hardly spend a nickel a word just to wire back that he couldn't remember you. Uncle John did know Longarm, as a U.S. deputy marshal on fairly friendly terms. But he was likely to either ignore a job application from a Dunk Crawford entire, or wire back that he had an opening. Riders were always coming and going at an outfit big as the Jingle Bob.

Slim Gonzales handed the yellow forms back, observing, ''You told Miss Connie you hadn't taken sides in that Lincoln County War.''

Longarm passed the forms across the counter to the clerk

with a nod of thanks as he replied to the lady's foreman, "Did I? I must have lied. Like I told her, things went to hell in a hack up Lincoln County way after Dad Peppin's posse and them colored troopers wiped out most of the Chisum, Tunstall, McSween shootists in the summer of '78. What I meant to tell Miss Connie was that I never gunned anybody for either side. Uncle John Chisum was only backing Lawyer McSween and his ad hoc Regulators with his dollars. He kept us Chisum *riders* herding Chisum *cows*, the way Major Murphy only funded the hired guns of Jim Dolan. I give you gents my solemn word I never pegged one shot at anybody, for anybody, during the Lincoln County War. I wasn't even working in or about the County Seat of Lincoln where most of the fights flared up."

He was smiling innocently as he told them that, for it was the pure unvarnished truth, however they might want to string it together.

The lean-and hungry-looking foreman turned to his boss wrangler to ask, "What do you think, Chongo?"

Chongo shrugged and said, "Miss Connie don't pay me to think. She tells me what she wants done and if it ain't impossible it gets done."

Gonzales nodded and said, "I reckon that's about the size of it."

Then he told Longarm, "You'd best come with us now. Our boss lady would like a word with you, and you just heard her described as our boss lady."

Longarm allowed he had nothing better to do, as long as they were talking about the Deveruex–Lopez town house. He explained he still had to stick around town until they held that coroner's inquest.

They didn't seem interested. They had a buckboard parked down the way in front of another saloon, so Longarm didn't have to fetch his own mount from the livery or walk all the way.

Chongo tethered the team out front, and that same snooty butler who got to sleep with the maids and likely the kitchen

120

help ushered them into that same big salon, where Consuela Deveruex y Lopez seemed to be holding court in yet another riding habit of summerweight shantung, the color of the 'dobe walls all around.

Longarm was pretending not to savvy much Spanish, so all his acting skills were called into play when she asked her foreman what he thought and Gonzales replied in Spanish that she was likely right about him.

It got tougher and he had to act surprised when she asked if they'd searched him and he had to wait until they told him in English that he could let them go through his pockets gently or risk some mighty rough handling at gunpoint if he made them call some others in to help.

Longarm thought it sensible to stare hard at the imperious dusky blonde as Chongo went through his pockets while she and Gonzales got to watch, with the *Tejano*'s bony brown hand hovering near the grips of his North & Savage .36-30. Chongo placed each item on the coffee table in front of the gal's uncomfortable but thronelike chair as he took them from Longarm's pockets. Longarm was sorry he hadn't been packing any rubbers. It would have served her right. He wasn't worried about the wallet, pocket knife, keys, comb, and such they were showing her because his badge, regular wallet, and field notes were hidden away with his arrest warrants. A man had to think ahead and you could hire a safe deposit box at any bank for a few cents a day. So he had, back at the county seat before he'd ever ridden into Sheffield Crossing.

Connie Deveruex took a folded wad of paper from the wallet he'd put together for Dunk Crawford and unfolded it before she quietly asked what a man who professed such a peaceful past might be doing with a reward poster in his peaceful pocket.

Longarm shrugged and said, "I told you I didn't know The Kid and I meant it when I said nobody seemed to know where he was right now. I never said I couldn't *use* that five-hundred dollar bounty, if things worked out that way."

Gonzales whistled softly and said, "You must think you're

pretty good. They say Billy The Kid has killed some people.''

Longarm asked, "Could I have my stuff back, now?"

The dusky blonde nodded and held his wallet up to him as with a smile to say, "You seem to be the New Mexico rider you said you were, Dunk Crawford. I'm still missing Greek Steve and we're getting set to drive a market herd to San Antonio. Do you still want a job?"

Longarm started putting things back in his pockets as he told her, "I just wired the Jingle Bob and swallowed some humble pie. I allowed I hadn't found the grass as green down this way as we'd been told. So with any luck they ought to wire back by the time your own coroner is done with me."

"Let me and my law firm worry about that coroner's inquest!" she cut in as if she was used to getting her own way. She said, "Hernando Nana was wanted dead or alive before you shot him. You may have some bounty money arriving by the time we get back, see?"

He shrugged and said, "I reckon. But didn't somebody tell me Greek Steve was on your payroll as a *wrangler*?"

She nodded and Chongo said, "He's on my crew. Or he was."

Longarm said, "I don't wrangle. I don't help the cook. And I don't ride drag. I ride as a top hand for forty-and-found or I don't ride at all, no offense."

She stared soberly up at him and said, "You *do* seem awfully sure of yourself. I usually start a rider at a dollar a day and see how things pan out. How are we supposed to know how good you are before we see how you ride?"

To which he replied without hesitation, "I just told you how I ride. How am I to know I'll get one red cent riding for anybody? I ain't seen any money, yet."

"Watch your mouth, cowboy!" snapped Slim Gonzalez.

But the dusky blonde just smiled up at Longarm and said, "That sounds fair. If you can't cut the muster on the trail I can always fire you, and if you don't think we're treating you right, you're free to quit. One of my younger *vaqueros* can

122

fill in for Greek Steve with the remuda. I suppose you only trail cows on point, Dunk Crawford?''

Longarm smiled and said, ''Aw, I ain't stuck-up, ma'am. I'll ride out front or off either swing, as long as you don't expect me to ride flanks or drag.''

He was hoping she'd tell him to go to hell. He'd been sent to track her kid brother down, not to herd her damned beef to San Antone. But she seemed amused by his cocky demands and said, ''*Bueno*, you'll start at forty-and found, and you'll be out on point with Slim and me, where I can keep an eye on you, starting out. If you last a full day, Slim here may want you riding swing.''

''*Right* swing,'' Longarm soberly insisted, adding, ''any fair rider can handle the *left* swing of a longhorn drive. You want someone better out on *right* swing.''

Chongo asked why. Longarm knew from the way Slim and his boss lady looked at one another that they'd both seen some stampeding on the trail. You had to know about such details if you aimed to sell your brags to real cow folk.

Consuela Deveruex y Lopez spit on her hand and held it out to her new rider. Longarm did the the same and they shook messy but for certain on their deal. Then she declared she meant to stay the night in town with her old momma, but she wanted the three of them to be out at the D Bar L, ready to ride, come sunrise.

So the three men left. Slim Gonzales waited until they were driving off in the buckboard, with Chongo holding the ribbons, before he told Longarm in an earnest tone, ''We're going to have to get a few things straight, here, cowboy. I am *El Segundo* of the D Bar L. So while you're working for Miss Connie you'll be taking your orders from me! Do you aim to give me any argument about that?''

Longarm said, ''Nope. You give me any orders you care to and as long as they're fit orders for a top hand I'll be proud to carry them out. If you hand me a shovel or ask me to fetch your pony for you, I won't. Do *you* have any argument about *that*?''

"I'm studying on it," Slim decided, adding, "How much gear do you have to load in the back and where's it at?"

Longarm said, "I've some baggage at the stage inn and I left my own pony, bridle, and saddle at the livery. Drop me off there and I'll be proud to get myself and all my shit out to the D Bar L on my own."

Slim said, "No you won't. Miss Connie's ordered our fence riders to treat any strange faces on her land as trespassers, and she's posted signs saying survivors will be prosecuted. So you'd best stay close to us until the others get to know you better."

Longarm shrugged and said, "I don't mind riding this buckboard in circles if you don't. But how come everyone's acting so proddy? They say Victorio's been driving off stock, but you've a big outfit a fair piece north of the border so . . ."

"We're not going to get along if you keep shitting me," Gonzales cut in, adding, "You know damn well who Miss Connie's worried about. You've been in these parts over an hour and it was you who shot one of Devil Dave's Mission Apache sidekicks last night!"

Longarm whistled softly and asked, "Are you saying she's scared of her own kid brother?"

It was Chongo who growled, "Wouldn't you be scared if you had a devil for a brother?"

Chapter 16

It was pushing midnight by the time Longarm reined in his buckskin by their buckboard at the D Bar L on the far side of the Pecos. Off in the darkness the occasional low of a cow and a mournful male voice crooning *La Paloma* off-key gave away the position of the bedded herd. Slim Gonzales had told him along the way they'd be driving around six hundred prime beef steers cut out of the main herd for slaughter. Thus the drive would be smaller but way friskier than "Dunk Crawford" might be used to. Longarm managed not to brag on driving that many cavalry mounts from behind enemy lines, after dark, in his day. But it wasn't easy.

The surly Chongo had insulted his range savvy along the trail by a tedious lecture on how he'd have to take the fresh pony they issued him from the remuda every morning. Longarm had told Chongo in passing that he didn't look down on *boss* wranglers. Any foreman had to know a heap about his job. Longarm had allowed he was sure the boss of the black gang on a steamboat knew more than he did about cordwood and boiler-water. But Chongo had still seemed pissed and anxious to show off his authority over the remuda.

Despite that sentimental yarn about Black Beauty, any rider who'd ever made a living on horseback knew nobody outside a novel or a half-ass history book rode one faithful mount, day after day. For a working beast of burden was really working, under a burden Mother Nature had never designed it for.

A horse living wild and free got to graze and gallop as the moment called for with no bit in its mouth and no saddle loaded with a full-grown man and his possibles on its back. So, like an athlete carrying on under more strain than a barefoot boy at play, any mount, and any cowpony in particular, had been through an equine version of a track meet or a day on a chain gang by the time it got to rest up and, like a human who'd been pushed about as hard as he could go, the critter tended to be tired the next day and stiff for three or four days more. So a serious cow hand rode a string of five to seven ponies with the bookkeeping easier when you made it seven. The boss wrangler, knowing more than the kids he had helping him care for the remuda, was the one who told you which pony you'd be riding if the boss had the bill of sale on the same. Riders naturally tended to like some ponies better. That was why the boss wrangler had the final say, lest hands wind up at odds over who got to ride what.

Chongo said that "Dunk Crawford" could ride his own buckskin any time he wanted, but suggested a fresh start on a fresh pony that knew the range, come morning. Longarm allowed he'd trailed cows all the way up the Midnight Loving Trail to Wyoming on a different pony every damned fool day. So Chongo growled, "Just so we understand one another."

Keeping *Tejano* hours, the boys in the bunkhouse were just fixing to turn in when Slim introduced Longarm to the bunkhouse crew and asked them to fix him up for a few hours of flop.

As soon as Slim left the strawboss, an Anglo of around forty, who they called Alamo, told Longarm he could spread his roll on a top bunk by the cold stove and said he'd wake him a tad early so's he could start out right.

When Longarm asked Alamo to clarify that, he was told all new hands got to swamp the bunkhouse floor whilst the others had breakfast. Old Alamo soothed, "You get to eat first, of course. Cooky will have you some fresh coffee, tor-

126

tillas, and beans to get you going before I wake up the rest of the boys."

Longarm smiled right back at the bunkhouse boss and said, "I don't know who you bet what, but you lose. I've signed on as a top hand, not a fucking swamper. Do you want to take it up at the big house or would you rather join me in a visit to fist city?"

Since few natural bullies made it to Alamo's age without knowing a mite about crawfishing, old Alamo laughed too loud and asked, "Can't you take a joke, Dunk? I never meant to have a top hand swamp a fool floor. I just wanted to see if you had a sense of humor."

Longarm knew others were listening, so he quietly declared, "I fear I don't. I don't laugh when some asshole short-sheets my bedroll and the last one who handed me a plate he'd heated over the campfire coals had to be driven in to the nearest town in a buckboard because he was in no shape to walk or ride, but he lived, and only walked with a slight limp when he got out of the hospital. I wouldn't want anyone to think I was a real sorehead."

So nobody else tested him that night. He unrolled his own bedding on the rope-sprung bunk they'd offered and didn't answer when the kid in the bunk below asked where he'd ridden before. So after a while he managed to catch a few winks, and then some silly son of a bitch was banging on a steel triangle and yelling, "Drop your cocks! Grab your socks! We got us some beef to carry to San Antone!"

So Longarm was just as glad he'd turned in fully dressed, save for his jacket, gunbelt, and boots. It was still dark out when he'd washed the gum out of his eyes at a latrine sink and ambled over to the cook house, where they were already lining up for breakfast.

Longarm was handed a confederate army mess kit and canteen cup to be served those promised tortillas and beans with fair black coffee. It had more chickory in it than they made coffee with as far north as the Texas Panhandle. But it had been brewed strong, so what the hell. When in Rome, or, in this case, close to the Gulf of Mexico, where they all seemed to think Creole tastes were so refined.

Longarm found a place to hunker and eat alone with his back braced against the cook house wall. He was minding his own business when a trio of *Tejano vaqueros* were looming over him, and the one with a shit-eating smile said, "Hey, gringo, for why you got on no *chaparreras*? Did not your mother tell you we have some chaparral to ride through between here and San Antonio?"

Longarm smiled up at them to gently but firmly reply, "My chaps are rolled up with my slicker. When and if I feel the need for either I'll just put them on with no advice from the drag riders, and if you ever mention my mother again I'll kill you. Are there any questions?"

The mouth of the testing trio tried, "I have one. Who do you think you just called a *chingado* drag rider? I am called El Moro and I ride *right swing*! You think I look like a drag rider, just because I am no gringo with big blue eyes and a little *piton*?"

"*No me jodas*, and you can ride any infernal position you want." Longarm sighed, hoping that would be the end of it.

It wasn't. El Moro suggested he stand up and repeat that remark about him being a lousy greaser riding drag.

Longarm didn't bite. The way the kid game of *Tu Madre* went involved an endless round of you-saids and no-I-didn't-say-exactly-thats as both sides felt one another out. Longarm had seldom seen a Border Mex of El Moro's ilk start anything before he'd felt his target out a lot.

So when El Moro asked for why he didn't get up, Longarm just told him he'd signed on to herd cows, not to swat flies.

"You call me a fly? You dare?" gasped El Moro.

Longarm shrugged and suggested, "If you ain't a fly, how come you're buzzing in my face for no damned reason? I ain't looking for trouble and I ain't afraid of you. If that ain't good enough for you, why don't we wait until we're off work in town and see who lives or dies? I wasn't hired to fight nobody this morning. Were you?"

El Moro grasped the straw and muttered "later" in a sullen tone as he led his two young pals away, still muttering.

The eastern sky was flamingo pink by then, and Captain Goodnight would have had his cows drifting out by the time you could see colors. But this outfit seemed in less of a hurry to saddle up. Longarm figured they might be worried about the beef stock being of the same age and mind. Cows moved more peaceable when you mixed their ages and genders as a herd in the wild might tally out. Young steers, like young boys, tended to be rowdy in large bunches.

Longarm let some of the others drift over to the corrals with their saddles and bridles to see what fate and Chongo had to offer. It was too late in the season for a West Texas dawn to be crisp. But it was cool enough for some of the rested up broncs to be feeling their oats, or, seeing it was West Texas, cracked corn.

Fueled by any fodder and well rested after their last hard day's work, some of the ponies expressed how they felt about another such day by bucking. El Moro rode his sun-fishing roan pretty good, Longarm had to allow. Then Chongo issued him a wall-eyed paint that didn't even want the bit in her mouth and a fine time was had by all before they had her bridled and saddled for Longarm to try out.

Since he was a new rider, the others took interest in the way he rode. Chongo's wranglers led all the riding stock out of the corrals and into the same ten-acre pasture before anybody mounted up to see how their rides for the coming day felt about them. So Longarm and the wall-eyed paint were having a heap of fun with one another when Connie Deveruex and Slim Gonzales reined in by the corral to watch.

The frisky paint mare had just settled down to a merry-go-round buck he found more tedious than challenging, so Longarm turned his toes out to dig those big Mex spurs in and hang on with them, making her hurt herself every time she shifted his weight, and, seeing they called it horse sense, she quit bucking.

Connie called out, "Not bad. That'll teach you to mean-mouth my wranglers, Dunk. Are you ready to ride?''

He rode the paint over to them and reined in to declare he felt as ready as he expected to get. Slim said, "The boys are forming up the herd, just past those blackjacks. We'll do better if the three of us swing wide and ride around instead of through them.''

Longarm said he'd ridden point before. So Slim took the lead and Longarm fell in to the left of his boss lady, riding sidesaddle in her fashionable habit and that flat Spanish hat.

He'd known gals who worked cows more manly, seated astride in a stock saddle with a throw rope and all. On the other hand, many a male boss never bothered learning to rope, for the same reasons planters named Jefferson or Lee seldom knew shit about chopping cotton. So it seemed moot whether Consuela Deveruex y Lopez knew how to rope and throw or not. Being the *owner*, she didn't *have* to. She could have been mounted on an elephant or sitting at home in a rocking chair and her beef would still be driven to market.

As they broke through the windbreak of oak trees Longarm saw there was indeed a long column of longhorns with calico hides headed into the sunrise and bitching about it some.

When you saw six hundred of anything spread out in a column four or five heads across it looked like more than you'd pictured. The three of them loped wide the length of the slowly moving column, and the drovers riding their own ponies at a walk, to fall in with the two *vaqueros* already out on point.

Whether you wanted to say you were leading or driving cows in large numbers the best ways to do so had been worked out by trial and error to fairly standard procedure.

You had point riders out just ahead of the lead critter, usually an older cow, called a bellwether by Anglo riders or a *madrastra* if you asked a Mex. Either way, such critters were never sold at the end of a drive and tended to get better at leading their fellow critters for their human drivers as time went on. Captain Goodnight kept a famous blue longhorn bellwether that would come when he called it.

Back to either side of the point, riders rode the swing riders, who could swing the column either way by crowding the head of it, but, as a rule, just tried to keep the lead cows bunched close and following the chosen route.

The flank riders trailed behind the swing riders down either side of the column to function much the same, save for having no say as to which way they were all going. Flank riders mostly kept stock from busting out of the herd to go in business on their own. A good flank rider never let a critter bust too far out of line. When he had to go tearing after them he wasn't a good flank rider, or else he was after a really bad critter. Young steers strayed worse than cows or calves with mommas. Nothing strayed worse than a doggie or orphan calf, and you hardly ever drove breeding bulls off their home ranges.

The necessary but unhappy drag riders brought up the rear, making certain no critters straggled as they got to ride through all the cow shit and most of the dust stirred up by the herd. It was the best chore for new students of the beef industry because you got to cope with the old and tired critters bringing up the drag instead of the wilder and meaner ones who tended to push forward. It was no accident that the word "bossy" came from an ancient word for cows.

As they followed what seemed a wagon trace through chaparral, Longarm saw they were setting a fair pace for beef on the hoof. He didn't ask why. This wasn't his first trail drive. He knew lots of trail bosses liked to move them as much as twenty-five miles the first day, albeit fifteen miles a day, or half the distance of a day's cavalry ride, was considered best for cows. Moving them fast and tight together at first was a fair way to trail-break or steady them down before you settled into a more comfortable steady drift, driving them some and grazing them some through the day and bedding them in a tighter bunch after dark when things went bump in the night and it was safer to circle and sing to them.

Seeing he had the chance and how they had so much more chapparal down this way, Longarm broke out the plain batwing chaps he'd brought from Denver and buckled them on as neither Connie nor Slim asked why. Professional chaps were made to be put on or off in the saddle without having to dismount. You had to put on shotgun chaps like pants. But he only had to buckle the batwings around his waist with a big floppy wing on either thigh and then simply snap the three fasteners down either thigh as far as the knees to be all set. But he was hoping he wouldn't have to ride through any of that sticker bush to the north or south as they drove ever onward into the sunrise under a cloudless sky that promised a West Texas scorcher.

He'd lit a cheroot and things were just settling down, perhaps two miles east of the Deveruex–Lopez home spread but still on their land grant when the low constant drumming of hooves was suddenly split by a single rifle shot.

One shot could be all that it took when six hundred young steers had never been given time to settle down. So Longarm didn't see why Connie Deveruex was yelling, "Stampede!" at the top of her lungs when anyone could see all hell was busting loose!"

Chapter 17

Longarm wheeled his wall-eyed paint to his right as he yelled at the gal seated sidesaddle to ride straight ahead at full gallop. He saw Slim Gonzales wheeling the other way. He'd thought old Slim knew which end of a longhorn the shit fell out of. He was mightly glad he'd slipped on his batwings as he and the paint left the trail at a dead run.

When you rode a horse through chaparral it looked after its own hide and you were supposed to look out for yourself. No horse with a lick of sense would tear through a thorn-lined gap too small for it to navigate. If its rider's legs were spread wider, no horse gave a shit. So the mesquite thorns to either side clawed considerable at the floppy leather armor of his chaps, as the heavier leather *tapaderas* covering his stirrups played hell with lower catsclaw, Spanish bayonet and such.

He spied that pain in the ass, El Moro, still being a pain in the ass out ahead as he waved his big sombrero and cussed at all those longhorns headed his way at full steam.

"*Pero no!* Fall back and try to get 'em to chase you!" Longarm yelled above the thunder of the oncoming hooves.

But El Moro had already proven he was a know-it-all with a chip on his shoulder so, even as Longarm galloped closer, El Moro reined in to stand his ground, waving his hat and cussing a blue streak as half a ton of beef, bone, and horn tore through a clump of prickly pear at him with its head down and its tail up in that mankilling arch young bullfighters are warned to watch out for.

Being neither a bullfighter nor a rider who listened to any-body about anything, El Moro was still sitting there like a big-ass bird when that first steer plowed his roan right out from under him. The startled Mex landed face down on the steer's powerful rump, bounced off, and landed on his boot heels smack in front of yet more beef on the thundering hoof. Then Longarm grabbed him by the scruff of his leather bolero in passing at full gallop and tore on through the chaparral half a furlong before the fresh-mouthed but hard-riding young Mex was up behind him, riding postillion as he hung on to Longarm as if they were long lost lovers in squaw boots.

Longarm yelled, "Hang on! I got me some rope to throw!"

El Moro gasped, "Have you been smoking funny *cigarillos*? They've spilled! There's no stopping that much *carne y hueso*, once it gets to moving!"

Longarm didn't answer as he shook out a loop, smaller than he might have if he hadn't been saddled with a backseat rider who kept telling him to get them both the hell out of there!

Then he'd overtaken the mean brute that had gored El Morro's roan and roped it by its right horn from its right side to inspire its whirling more to the right in a clockwise attempt to gore the wall-eyed paint, this time.

But for all her bucking, the paint was still an old cowpony who'd been trained to keep the rope taught betwixt its sad-dlehorn and an object of any sort doing anything at the other end of said rope. So El Moro was screaming in sheer terror and Longarm was laughing like a loon as the two men rode one of the two beasts in a mad kerchief dance through mes-quite and a whole lot of rising dust, as other beef circled in like soap bubbles swirling down the drain hole of a bath tub until, having no drain hole to swirl down, they just circled the central swirl in confusion.

"We're milling them!" El Moro yelled in a happier tone

as the big steer trying to gore the paint gave up to just hang there at the far end of the taut hemp, head down and tongue hanging way out as it pawed dust to prove it was still out to win, as soon as it figured this fool game out.

Longarm had no call to explain to a cowboy how stampeding cows were inclined to stampede clockwise. Longarm didn't know why most men were right handed, either. But he'd never seen cattle stampede the other way, counterclockwise, and once you had them milling in a circle, they were as good as standing in one place, save for all the weight they were out to lose on you as they panted and puffed with horns clashing.

By this time other D Bar L riders had circled in on all sides to bunch the mill tighter, and as the herd steadied down to a milling walk Longarm saw there was no handy way to get that steer off the other end of his rope from the saddle. So he told the Mex behind him, "I paid good money for that rope and that steer can't have it. Take these reins and scoot your crotch forward as I dismount, hear?"

El Moro gasped, "You can't be serious! Those brutes charge a man on foot on sight!"

Longarm allowed he'd have to teach 'em better manners. He threw his right leg across the horn in front of them to sit sidesaddle just long enough to hand the reins to El Moro. Then he only had to draw his left boot from the stirrup to drop lightly to the dust and go hand-over-hand along the rope as the steer on the far end eyed him wildly, trying to solve a problem it had never been offered before.

Then Longarm muttered, "Oh boy!" as he saw that tail going back up to arch just above its roots with the bushy end whipping back and forth like a cobra trying to line up on a swaying Hindu and his pesky flute. That long rack of horns went down. Longarm tried to decide which way he wanted to dodge as he remembered reading how no Spanish bullfighter would face this mongrel breed because you just never knew with a longhorn, bred for nothing better than stringy supper grub.

135

Then another shot rang out and the crazed critter simply dropped as if it had already made it to the sledge-man at the San Antone slaughter house.

Longarm glanced to his right to see Connie Deveruex demurely seated sidesaddle with a smoking Navy .36 in one dainty hand as she called out, "Get your rope and get back in your saddle, you silly! That brute cost me a good pony and Lord knows how much trail wastage. The one's left ought to be easier to manage, now. What was that noise that set them off like that? It sounded like a rifle shot."

Longarm said, "It was, ma'am. Let me ride El Moro, here, back to his own saddle and I'll see what we can find out."

He got his rope free and rode with the Mex to a roan pounded flat in a patch of trampled mesquite and cheat. He reined in and said, "Your saddle ain't busted up too bad, and your saddlebags should have gotten your possibles through."

As the younger *Tejano* dropped off, he stared around to soberly declare, "*Jesus, Maria y Jose!* I think you just saved my life, gringo!" Longarm modestly replied, "I know I did. Don't call me gringo if you don't want me calling you greaser, El Moro."

The *Tejano* smiled up at him boyishly to reply, "Is a deal. *Como se llama?*"

Longarm allowed Dunk would do well enough and left the dismounted *Tejano* by his battered horse and saddle for the remuda riders, bringing up the rear behind the chuck wagon, to cope with at their own pace.

That mysterious rifle shot was the real question before the house.

Rejoining Connie Deveruex near the dead steer, he spied Slim Gonzales and two other D Bar L hands escorting an Anglo in bib overalls and a straw hat, mounted on a mule, in from the North. Gonzales was holding a twenty-gauge shotgun high in his free hand as he rode within earshot to call, "This one claims he was hunting quail, Miss Connie. If you'd care for my opinion he was after a free side of beef!"

The dusky blonde stared imperiously at the scared and nei-

136

ther too young nor too bright-looking Anglo as she declared, "Whatever you were hunting, you were hunting it on my land, Mister. Might you have the price of one good cow pony and one prime steer on you this morning?"

The scared old coot whined, "I never shot no pony! I never shot no steer! I pegged one shot at an infernal quail and I missed! Nobody told me I was on private land, ma'am. I just rode south from my government claim to see if I could put us some game meat on the table, and I never seen no posted property signs!"

Slim Gonzales said, "We've put 'em up plain every quarter mile and cleared a fence line we mean to string wire along one of these days. We know the damn yankee Federal Land Office has thrown open all that grazing land to you homesteading pests, north of the county line. Just like you were told, anything this side of it was the Deveruex-Lopez Land Grant."

He turned to his boss lady and asked, "What do you want us to do with him, Miss Connie?"

She looked undecided and allowed she was open to suggestions. One of the *Tejanos* who'd rounded him up with Gonzales volunteered, "Why don't you take his mule, scattergun, and boots in partial payment and let us escort him off your property, Miss Connie?"

Another suggested, "Why escort him when we can rope and drag him? Being drug half that far would surely impress most nesters with the need to pay attention to property lines."

She turned to Longarm to ask, "What do you think, Dunk?"

Longarm didn't think he ought to say he felt sorry for the poor old greenhorn, who likely needed that one mule he owned in this world.

So he said, "Only one way to deal with him, Miss Connie. Ain't none of this mesquite tall enough for his toes to clear the ground. But we ain't too far from them blackjack oaks to hang him right."

It worked. It was Slim Gonzales who objected that solution

137

might cause more trouble than the dead stock was worth. It was the hand who wanted to drag a man miles through chaparral who said flat out that he wasn't willing to take part in any murder.

As there came an uneasy murmur of agreement, Connie said, "I can see how things got out of hand up Lincoln County way if your old boss dealt with *trespassers* so . . . permanently!"

Longarm shrugged and said, "You never heard me say I'd seen anybody hanging from a tree on Jingle Bob range, Miss Connie. I only answered your question as best I knew how. Nobody trespasses on the Jingle Bob. Some say that's because Uncle John's riders hang unwelcome riders from the nearest tree and others say such pests just vanish into thin air with their final fates unknown. I told you when you asked that I never killed a soul for anybody when I was drawing forty-and-found for working cows and working cows alone!"

She insisted, "You just now offered to kill this poor nester for me, didn't you?"

Longarm just shrugged and asked, "If you don't want us to hang him for you, what *do* you want us to do with him, Miss Connie?"

He liked her better when she snapped. "Oh, just get the *pendejo* out of my sight this time, and make certain he understands things won't go as easily on him the next time!"

Slim Gonzales told his two Mex followers, in Spanish, to escort the nester off the grant and just rough him up a little to make sure he understood exactly where the property lines might be.

Longarm pretended not to understand. As a sworn peace officer he'd have been honor-bound to step in if they'd really meant to adminster cruel and unusual punishment without a fair trial. But, seeing the old greenhorn could use a little help with his own disregard of common law, Longarm was sure Billy Vail would go along with a split lip or a black eye.

As the *vaqueros* led the trespasser north through the chap-

138

arral, the owner of the milled and bunched beef asked Long-arm, "I suppose you think I'm a sissy?"

Longarm grinned at her and replied, "Being sort of sissy ain't no shame to a lady of quality, ma'am. What do you want us to do about your remaining cows?"

She laughed and said, "Let them graze and settle down some more before we drift them back into line on the trail and move them out again."

She turned to her *segundo* to ask, "Isn't that the way you see it, Slim?"

Gonzales nodded, agreed in English, but added softly in Spanish, "These cattle are not the only wild animals we may have to deal with between here and San Antonio. I warned you this one could be a paid assassin!"

She told Slim to let her worry about that and turned back to Longarm to tell him, in English, "We won't be here long enough to brew a round of coffee. But I think we could all use something stronger after all that excitement. Ride back to the chuck wagon with me and I'll stand you to a shot of tequila."

Longarm didn't argue, but as the two of them walked their ponies to the west he noticed Slim wasn't tagging along. It wasn't for him to ask how come. But she said she'd told Slim to drift their *madrasta*, or bellwether, back to the trail and see how many others naturally took to grazing nearby. He hadn't expected her to tell him Slim had called him a paid assassin.

Passing the place where El Moro's roan had gone down, its owner pointed with her riding crop to say, "I saw what you did for El Moro over there. I doubt the hide of that poor roan would be worth salvaging, but we're still close enough to my home spread to send word about that dead steer."

Longarm saw El Moro out ahead, trudging alongside the trail with his saddle braced on one hip. You trudge *beside* a recently traveled cattle trail unless you admired cowshit on your boots.

Gazing about at her grazing cattle he refrained from com-menting on all that mesquite, accusing her of overgrazing, but casually asked just how far east her family grant extended.

She said, "We'll be camping on D Bar L range tonight and the night after. But in God's truth our grant is not as large as some think. All such ranchos near all-year water were laid out as *cintas* with their narrow dimensions facing the rivers so that all might have plenty of water as well as plenty of land. I don't know why New Mexico let John Chisum claim so much range north and south along the upper Pecos. It makes his Jingle Bob look so big, next to the really bigger Spanish grant of Lucien Maxwell."

He figured she was testing him some more. So he kept his voice as casual when he replied, "Begging your pardon, ma'am. Old Lucien died five summers back and it's his son, Pedro, grazing them close to two million acres these days. We call him Pete Maxwell, and he's a good old boy. But, for the record, the Maxwell Grant ain't Spanish. Old Lucien bought out the heirs of Don Guadalupe Miranda and a French-Canadian mountain man called Beaubien or Pretty Good, and they'd been granted the land in Apache Country by Old Mexico, not the earlier kings of Spain. I reckon I'd best give yon *vaquero* a hand with his saddle."

She didn't object as he called ahead to El Moro, who swung around with a weary smile to wait up for them. Long-arm had learned how to get suspects to talk since he'd been riding with old Billy Vail. It seemed natural to clam up when somebody asked you right out what you had on your mind. It got tougher to keep a secret when nobody seemed to think you had one, and they had many a mile to go before they were even off her land. So he felt no call to ask her right out why she seemed to be in the market for a hired killer.

Chapter 18

The drive took the better part of two weeks and they all had a heap more time than Longarm or Billy Vail had planned on to get to know one another. Albeit nobody in the outfit seemed to know Connie Deveruex in the Biblical sense, and Longarm doubted he was the only rider waking up alone in a bedroll with a hard-on by the second or third morning on the trail.

They'd driven the herd a hard seventy-five miles in the first three days to trail-break them. Then Slim set the pace closer to fifteen miles a day, lest they wind up with a lot less beef on the hoof by the time they got to the buyers in San Antone.

But even knowing beef sold by the pound, Longarm was a heap more anxious than their owner to see the last of their dusty hides in San Antone. Her crazy-mean kid brother hadn't joined them along this trail as hoped. He might or might not be waiting on the sale of all this beef to grubstake a serious trip to distant climes. Longarm knew Devil Dave's big sister could have sold the beef for way more up North in Nebraska, where the rails fed the crowded industrial East. But he couldn't risk asking her why she was willing to settle for less money faster. It was possible the numbers added up much the same, once you tallied the costs of a longer drive and rail freight charges in with a quicker sale in San Antone.

He'd have asked a lady her real age before he'd ask the price she'd be asking or how much beef she still had grazing off to the west. He'd been raised too polite and he knew no *Tejano* counted stars or cows. Or so they said.

Earlier in that same century this would have been true. English-speaking folk were beef eaters. Spanish speakers ate pigs or chickens when they could afford to and considered beef a second-rate by-product of the leather, soap, and bull-fight traders.

Up until the Mexican War, the Hispano-Moorish longhorn cattle of the Southwest had roamed half wild on the range they could get by on, whilst their owners worried more about such profitable stock as horses, mules, poultry, and swine because they all needed more attention.

Brush-popping cows, living more like deer out on marginal range, had been rounded up from time to time and butchered for their hides and tallow. Cowhide tanned cheap, to superior leather, whilst cow tallow made so-so candles and the fine Spanish soap sold as "Castile," but even the first Anglo-Texicans had left most of the meat to rot because there just hadn't been any way to get more than a little jerked beef to the eastern market before the post-war railroad boom.

Things were way different with business back East driving the price of beef ever higher, and even the Potato Famine Irish were able to afford corned beef and cabbage more than once a month. So the despised free-ranging cow now stood supreme as the livestock of the West, and it was the poor Mex or Anglo homesteader you saw raising pigs and chickens for market these days. For even *Tejanos*, trying to display as much high tone as their Anglo rivals, had taken to serving steak and potatoes in the bigger towns such as El Paso or San Antone.

Longarm, having proven his worth in that first stampede, rode mostly right swing and prevented a stampede or more by keeping a sharp eye on the natural troublemakers in the lead and moving in fast to herd them back in place and pace with

142

the morse sensible cows. The knack was in knowing when to
wave and cuss and when to join a jailbreak as it was starting
and see if you could get them to follow you in a circle-dance
whilst the left swing rider yelled and fired off his sixgun to
the outside of your circle. Any cow hand who yelled whoopy-
skippy at a herd that was behaving would have been fired and
encouraged to take up life upon the wicked stage in one of
those Wild West shows.

So Longarm was just walking his pony of the day at a
steady two-miles-an-hour stroll a sparking couple could have
managed along any garden path when he noticed Connie and
Slim up ahead, reined in to talk to a cluster of strange riders
sitting their own mounts in a line across the trail. They were
all dressed more Anglo than Mex, albeit the styles of the
vaquero and the buckaroo, pronounced much the same,
tended to blend into one another by degrees, and you had to
watch who you called a greaser in West Texas.

Longarm waved the flank rider behind him forward and
told the kid to hold the milled and grazing lead cows where
they were as he rode ahead in time to hear one of the Texicans
calling Slim Gonzales a greaser. So he drew his Winchester
'73 from its saddleboot and put it across his thighs as he
walked his pony to join the party with an inquiring smile.

None of the ragged-ass riders smiled back as they regarded
him with as much curiosity. He read their outfits as trash
white with delusions of grandeur. Real cow hands seldom
wore baggy pants or suspenders, and none of them had throw-
ropes on their saddle swells.

Falling in to Connie's right, since Slim had reined in to her
left as a *segundo* was supposed to, Longarm kept his eyes on
the full-bearded obvious leader of the half dozen strangers as
he calmly declared, "The boys asked me to find out why
we've stopped here, ma'am."

Connie's voice wasn't half so calm as she replied, "That's
the topic under discussion at the moment, Dunk. These gentlemen seem to feel we don't have the right-of-way across
open range. These gentlemen must be weary of life."

Longarm went on smiling as he stared at the bearded one to observe, "Aw, it ain't that hot this afternoon. I'm sure these gents have some reason for being so confused. Do I have your permit to talk to them?"

Slim spoke out from her far side, "We've gotten past talking, Dunk. I just told them, polite, we had the guns and the grit to keep going whether they liked it or not and they called me a durned greaser and dared us to try!"

Longarm repeated, "Ma'am?" and she nodded, so Longarm walked his pony forward, calling out, "Howdy, I'd be Dunk Crawford from Lincoln County and you'll find me as easy to get along with as you'll let me."

Nobody answered until he reined in close to the bearded one, who grudgingly said, "I'd be Hamp Morrison and you ain't driving all them damned cows over the next rise behind us because we're trying to grow some damned barley and we'll not have it trampled!"

Longarm nodded pleasantly and said, "We'd heard the land office has opened up more government range to homesteading. Could you and me ride off a piece for a more private conversation, Mister Morrison?"

The appointed leader of the homesteaders demanded, "Why? Ain't one thing we could say that I don't want the whole world to hear."

"I can see you ain't never been married up." Longarm smiled, adding with a meaningful glance, "There's some things best said man-to-man that a lady's ears might find offensive."

It worked. As Connie stared thunderghasted, the burly Morrison gave in to his own curiosity and rode north with Longarm until the two of them were in sight but out of the hearing range of the tense confrontation on the cattle trail.

Longarm reined in first to say, "I just hate to talk about cow shit in front of ladies. Don't you?"

Morrison swung his farm plug closer as he scowled and demanded, "You brought me over here to talk about cow shit?"

Longarm nodded and added, "Dry cow shit. Prairie peat. Texas coal. Burns slower than wood and I see you've already cleared a lot of the mesquite you found in these parts. You gents do have your new homesteads fenced, don't you?"

Morrison said, "Not entirely. We chipped in for a drift fence along this infamous cattle trail. But the point is that cattle stray and our spring-planted barley has barely sprouted, temping as vanilla ice cream to your average cow!"

Longarm nodded sagely and said, "That's the truth. You were smart to drill in barley. Too dry out this way for wheat or corn. You'll want to raise some chicken and pigs as soon as you settle in some, too. Farming this far west of the Brazos without irrigation can be a bitch."

Morrison looked more worried than angry now, as he sighed and said, "Tell me something I'd have never guessed. You see how it is. We just can't have cattle crossing our hard-won crop lands!"

Longarm asked, "Ain't there no open range left outside that drift fence you just mentioned?"

The farmer nodded but said, "There is. But it's rough range indeed and you'd never get a goat to stay on it if there were barley sprouts in plain sight behind three strands of bob!"

Longarm nodded some more, but insisted, "We ain't driving goats to San Antone. We're herding cows with more riders than you really want to tangle with and, wait, don't get your shit hot until I've finished, said riders can make better friends than enemies if you not only get out of their way but invite Miss Consuela Deveruex y Lopez over for coffee and cake whilst she beds her herd across the way for the night. Anyone can see it'll soon be sundown and . . ."

"You're crazy," Morrison cut in.

Longarm insisted, "I'd rather be called crazy than just plain stupid. You ain't going to win if you try to bar a public right of way. I doubt like hell you could stop Miss Connie and the rest of us. But even if you could there'd be others, and *vaqueros* don't just bed cows down after dark. They've been known to burn unwelcome neighbors out."

145

"Are you threatening us with night riding?" the burly homesteader demanded.

To which Longarm replied in a firm but friendly tone, "Don't have to. Don't want to. As a man with Miss Connie's interests at heart I'd be first to advise her to just go around you unfriendly folk. It would mean an extra half day on the trail but likely less trouble with the rangers. The rangers can be such fusses about a little arson or gunplay. Other cattle outfits might or might not go around you. Whether they did or not, like I said, you've cut all the handy mesquite and you'll be giving up a hell of a lot of free fuel! One herd bedded down overnight can leave wagon loads of cow chips, each about the size of a saucer and ready to burn like Irish peat, with less stink, once it dries out total under this Texas sun."

It worked. As he'd hoped, the hard-scrabble homesteader had already cut and cured enough mesquite to grasp the advantages of an easier to to gather fuel. He cautiously asked, "You have enough riders to keep them north of the trail and nowhere else?"

Longarm smiled modestly and replied, "I'm paid to ride swing and not let 'em go anwhere without permission."

So they rode back to their comrades-in-arms on the trail and the burly Morrison called out, "War's over, boys! I'll tell you about the deal as we ride home."

Then he turned to Connie to tug at his hat brim and add, "My wife would doubtless be proud to coffee and cake you if you'd care to stop by this evening, Miss Deveruex. Our place is the first one over yonder rise, with the patent windmill and the scarecrow wearing a red shirt."

Then he wheeled his old plug to ride after his younger pals as the dusky blonde stared in wonder after him.

Longarm said, "He invited your visit because there's a handy cleared patch to bed the herd, across from his spread, with night coming on. But I reckon we could drive 'em a few miles further if you want, Miss Connie."

She asked, "What did you say to him, just now? He didn't seem the least scared of Slim, here."

Slim muttered in Spanish, "I have no reputation as a murderer."

Longarm pretended not to understand as he told Connie, "We just talked it over, ma'am. I've found you can talk your way out of lots of trouble if you choose your words with care."

Slim Gonzales smiled thinly and said, "I used to know an *hombre* who could talk bankers out of money by choosing his words with care. He said, 'Stick 'em up!'. The last I heard he was serving time in state prison."

Longarm laughed lightly and replied, "Some of us have the gift whilst others don't. It's like shooting pool."

Slim asked, "Did you offer to shoot him in a pool?"

Connie said they'd best move her herd on to that bedding ground. So Longarm loped back to the right swing position and they did as she asked. It took less than a full hour before they had her beef spread across the glorified weed-lot across the trail from the three strands of drift wire and the four quarter-section homesteads to the south. A little gal in bib overalls and pigtails came across to ask Connie to sup with her folks before the sun went down. Longarm hunkered with the other D Bar L riders around the chuck wagon crew's coffee fire to sup on grits and gravy with chicken enchiladas. Tex-Mex cooking could get like that. He went easy on the coffee, not having drawn night duty and having ever more trouble falling asleep alone, as one lonesome night followed another out here amid all this nothing-much. But as he hunkered there watching the sunset, whilst cows lowed all around and somebody got to strumming a sad Mex tune on a distant guitar, Longarm was reminded of something he'd read about East India and the way they called the gloaming "The hour of cow dust," which made them Hindu cowhands sound as poetic as your average Mex with a guitar.

Then it was deep purple with the stars winking on, and Longarm and his bedroll drifted upwind to a patch of love

147

grass nothing had been grazing or shitting on. He was spreading his bedding on the vanilla-scented grass when Connie crossed the road from the Morrison spread, spied him there, and came over to declare, "When you scare men they do stay scared! I wasn't able to get a thing out of Farmer Morrison just now. To hear him talk, you'd think the two of you had gone in business together!"

Longarm smiled up at her to say, "We have. Sort of. I convinced him it was better business to make friends with passing cow outfits than it was to pick fights with them."

The dusky blonde stamped a boot heel and said, "Don't be such a big fibber. You scared the liver and lights out of the whole bunch and why won't you tell us what you said to make such a sea change in that big mean Anglo? Are you afraid we'd tell the law on you, Dunk?"

Longarm managed not to laugh. But it wasn't easy as he soberly said, "Ask me no questions and I'll tell you no lies, Miss Connie. We all have our own little secrets and you don't hear me asking you about anything you wouldn't want the law to know about, do you?"

Chapter 19

Longarm had been riding six or eight years for the law. So he'd almost forgotten how much the daily grind of the cow hand reminded him of being in the army. They got you up early and let you off for the day late, when you didn't draw night duty. The cow hand got more pay, but the army served somewhat better grub and issued you the duds and gear a cowboy had to buy out of his own pocket. After that, in both cases, you spent hours of boredom punctuated by mighty exciting moments and, the hell of it was, you didn't want to let your guard down when nothing was happening because you never had much warning things were fixing to blow, and you didn't want to be caught gathering moon beams when they did.

They were driving the herd across the Edwards Plateau, and "plateau" was French for a flat stretch, which the Edwards Plateau lived up to as tedious as it could manage. So day after day went much the same as they drifted the same damned herd through what seemed like the same damned miles and miles of little more than miles and miles.

But all those miles and miles provided more than enough space for an occasional something else. They had to ford what seemed the same chocolate-colored stream once or twice a day, and every other day or so they'd find themselves within sight of what seemed the same lights of the same trail town, with little more than a few shop signs and new faces to tell them they hadn't ridden in a big circle.

Cows didn't take kindly to surprises. So you let the sunrise wake them natural and gave them some time to water and graze, if there was anything wetter than dew nearby. Then you took your sweet time drifting them into line and moving them out some more.

When you came to water you let them scatter some and drink their fill because, like other grazing critters, they could store a bodacious heap of water in their guts or draw on body fat betwixt drinks, which sold by the pound at the end of the trail.

Moving at the pace of a courting couple most of the time, you let them break trail and graze a spell every three miles or when you came upon good grass. There wasn't too much of that along a cattle trail by this late in the green-up, and a lot more mesquite and pear had crowded in where the buffalo had once kept the lawn mowed more neatly.

You wanted to move them well off the trail and bed them in a rounder bunch before sundown got the snakes and skittersome critters of Rattlesnake Time broke cover as the shadows lengthened. You never left a trail herd untended off its home range. But Slim Gonzales saw no reason to have more than one rider at a time slowly circle them after dark to assure them there were no wolves about and to give the alarm if there were. So, save for the two nights when it was cloudy in the East and threatening thunder, most of the small outfit got to ride into any town within reach after a day in the saddle.

An occupational disease you never read about in Ned Buntline's Wild West magazines plagued the cowboy, or cowgal riding for hours astride a warm smooth saddle. Victorian folk who had to ride a lot, east or west, well knew of which they spoke when they allowed no proper young lady ought to ride astride, with her maidenly crotch open to the warm and constant caress of a saddle in motion under her until who knew *what* temptations might be popping into her innocent young head?

Cavalrymen and cowboys, having no choice but to ride astride as they rode more serious, just had to put up with the mild but constant crotch massage until they could dismount someplace where the local gals understood the natural natures of men on horseback.

Fathers, brothers, and swains of some such gals knew exactly what a stranger riding in after sundown was after before he settled down for some serious drinking and card playing. So, riding with a smaller than usual outfit, Longarm, Slim, Chongo, Cooky, and some of the other grown men of the D Bar L had to step in fast to nip trail-town brawls in the bud by hauling a younger rider away from some scandalized town-twist or buying her big brother a drink.

The older and wiser men of such towns, in turn, were as anxious to head off trouble and keep things friendly. For most every merchant and saloon keeper in the West had heard the sad tale of Abilene, the one in Kansas, where Marshal Tom Smith from the New York City Police had made a name for himself as a town tamer and brought financial ruin to the town.

In 1868 seventy thousand head of cattle had been shipped East from Abilene. Smith had been appointed marshal in '70, and in '71 not a cow or Texas cowboy bothered anyone in Abilene worth mention. The welcome signs and newspaper ads in Texas papers that followed were just wasted money. The wide-open town of Newton was served by the Santa Fe and a tad closer to Texas when you studied on it. So it was now considered dumb to make cow outfits study on whether to ride in or ride around, and this tended to keep things under control.

Longarm was able to calm a couple of tense situations that Slim had to admit he'd needed help with. Most of the dozen-odd *Tejano* riders in the outfit were good old boys, Anglo or Mex, who only wanted to let off a little steam when the got near expensive whiskey and cheap women. But El Moro and his two more constant sidekicks, Pablo and Latigo, could get tense indeed with anybody. Longarm had been given an early taste of El Moro's annoying swagger, and seen how the kid played to the audience he led around to watch him do his stuff. But, having saved El Moro's hide that time, Longarm had an edge even Slim didn't have, once the natural bully was strutting his stuff.

El Moro seemed to like him. It was simple as that. The three of them combined couldn't have mustered the common sense of an average prize fighter, seeing they picked fights for no prize at all, but the spite-filled El Moro seemed driven by the simple fact that nobody had ever been nice to such a dedicated pain in the ass. So he'd been overwhelmed by Longarm's common decency and seemed to think Longarm loved him, albeit in a manly way.

This caused Longarm no concern at first. He had way more important things to worry about, he thought, than whether he was popular with Miss Connie's hired help. The two of them had gotten to talk a heap after more than a week on the trail, and Longarm was almost sure she was sending smoke signals with those big old hazel eyes, unless he was simply too hard-up to lock eyes with a gal and not think about her more private parts.

In either case, he hadn't been able to get a thing about her kid brother out of her and that seemed only fair, since he hadn't told her who he was really riding for, either.

Choosing not to buddy up with any other D Bar L rider in particular, Longarm was free to duck into a trail town Western Union now and again to get off a one-way wire to Marshal Billy Vail by way of his typist in the unlikely event Connie Deveruex still had Chongo watching him. The boss wrangler appeared to have lost interest in him, once he'd shown he could ride and Miss Connie had allowed he could ride along.

He asked his boss to wire him in care of the main Western Union office in San Antone if they'd found out anything about anybody back in Denver, or just wanted him to pack it in.

It went that way sometimes. There was never a pony that couldn't be rode, never a rider that couldn't be throwed, and nobody won every time. The rangers hadn't been able to cut Devil Dave's trail. He hadn't been able to cut Devil Dave's trail, and how could they be sure there was any trail to cut?

He could see that no kid brother, with or without that mysterious Hogan, could ride with his big sister and this modest outfit. Nobody had been able to find him holed up in Sheffield-Crossing or out on his home spread. It was just as likely he'd never come home, this time, or come by long enough to beg, borrow, or steal enough to move on, perhaps on down the Pecos where it met the Rio Grande on the Mexican border. It would serve the mean little shit right if he met up with Victorio and, come to study on it, those two sidekicks accounted for had been Apache, or Mission Apache, least ways. Knowing how to speak the complicated lingo of the NaDéné nations could make all the difference when you met up with the ones called Apache, or "Enemies" in the Uto-Aztec dialects of most other Southwest nations. The folk who called themselves NaDéné, or natural folk, had drifted down from the far North, speaking a lingo unrelated to any other, and hard as hell to learn. So they were used to robbing, raping, and killing others, red or white, with little or no conversation and thus, when they did meet up with anybody who could howdy them, it confused the shit out of them and they had to study on what happened next.

Old Captain Tom Jeffords, a steamboat skipper hired to supervise the Overland mail through Apacheria back about the time Marshal Smith was taming Abilene, had taken the time and trouble to learn some baby talk NaDéné so's he could hire an Apache friendly to take him into see Cochise and ask him what all the fuss was about. The notion that a white eyes was willing and able to talk to him astonished Cochise to where they decided to call Jeffords *Taglito* because he had a red beard, and leave his mail riders alone because he asked them to.

But the notion of Devil Dave and some Mission Apache

breed joining forces with Victorio hardly promised better mail delivery!

Such grim notions tended to strengthen Longarm's doubts about Devil Dave being anywhere closer. Then, one evening as they were camped on a lonely expanse with nothing to ride into after work but pear flats, Connie Deveruex got Longarm and his supper off to one side to say they had to talk.

Longarm allowed he was willing as they sat on the rim of a wash with their boots dangling and their mess kits in their laps, canteen cups of coffee on the stubble between them, as if to keep him from rubbing his hip against her own.

A man got mighty aware of shemale hips after all those days in the saddle if he was too fastidious for the modest offerings of trail town whorehouses.

Connie said, "Somebody told me you knew Irene Pantages, back there in Sheffield-Crossing."

Longarm knew how complicated a web you could weave when you lied more than you really had to. So he just nodded and said, "I do. She's a dressmaker. She told me she runs sheep over to the west and she asked me if I knew where her cousin by marriage, Greek Steve, might be. I told her true as I'm telling you, I have no idea where Greek Steve went or why he felt so inclined. I didn't know him. I didn't ask him where he was going. So he never told me."

The dusky blonde stared into the last rays of the sunset on the dead-flat western horizon as she said in a matter-of-fact voice he suspected she was putting on, "It must have taken a lot of words to convince her. They tell me you spent the whole night with her."

Longarm picked up his cup and sipped some coffee as he thought back and chose his words with care before he replied, "That ain't so, ma'am. Whoever told I spent the night there is a liar and I'd be proud to say so to his face. Miss Irene served me some refreshings and sheltered me from the cruel sun during the worse afternoon heat but . . ."

"I stand corrected. It was the long cozy *siesta* time you

154

spent in bed with that Greek cow!'' the more petite *Tejana* blazed.

Longarm sipped more coffee, put his cup down betwixt their hips, and calmly said, ''I didn't know Chongo was peering through the keyhole. What Miss Irene and me might or might not have done in the privacy of her own home ain't nobody else's beeswax, no offense. So what do you care whether I spent a night, a *siesta*, or a whole blamed year sipping tea or rutting like a hog with another lady entire?''

Connie grimaced and decided, ''That's a disgusting picture to contemplate. I don't really care what you and that sheepherding dressmaker might have done, as you just said, in private. But her cousin did ride for me. He does seem to be missing, and she must have thought you knew something about it. Was that why she seduced you, to make you talk, you poor thing?''

Longarm started to deny the whole affair. Then he wondered why a man might want to lie when the truth might work out in his favor. So he smiled sheepishly and confessed, ''She thought I might be a lawman.''

The dusky blonde turned to him with a puzzled frown to demand, ''She suspected you were the law? We all know Greek Steve thought you'd said something to the rangers about him.''

Longarm nodded and said, ''That, too. Miss Irene told me Greek Steve told her he had to get out of town because he was in trouble with the law. She sent for me because I'd been seen talking to a ranger just after Greek Steve left town and just before the rangers rode out after him, or perhaps Victorio. That's who they told me they were after. Do you reckon Greek Steve rode off to join the Apache Nation, ma'am?''

She seemed to be choosing her own words when she answered in a way too casual tone, ''I've no idea what Stavros Pantages was worried about. Might his cousin have offered any suggestions?''

Since, for all he knew, the two gals had been comparing notes on him, which had happened in the past, Longarm truthfully replied, "She did say he'd told her he'd done something unlawsome, and been asked to do something worse. He never told her what he'd done or who was after him to do worse."

She sipped some of her own coffee in the gathering dusk whilst she studied that. Then she demanded, "That was it? That was all either of you knew and you wound up in bed together?"

Again Longarm smiled sheepishly and confessed, "Both of use were young and healthy. But if the full truth be known, somebody had told Miss Irene I wouldn't even kiss her if I was really a lawman. So she may have had that in mind, too."

The dusky blonde was getting tougher to see by then. So he couldn't read her pretty face as her voice grew sort of husky as she asked if that could be true.

Longarm honestly replied, "What are we talkling about, ma'am? Lawmen not being allowed to make love to gals they meant to arrest or even call to testify? You'd have to ask a lawman or a lawyer about that, ma'am. Miss Irene seemed convinced I couldn't arrest her after a little slap-and-tickle, and I can't deny I never arrested her. Does that make me an undercover lawman a pretty gal can wrap around her finger, or saddle tramp who got lucky?"

Connie laughed and said, "You ought to be ashamed of yourself, you big goof. What has that Greek cow to offer that I can't top with room to spare?"

Longarm said, "I can't say. Are you offering?"

She didn't answer. She jumped up and ran off in the dark. A lot of gals were like that, damn it all to hell.

Chapter 20

The last sunset on the trail found them on the banks of the San Antonio River with the lights of San Antone winking on the horizon. So they bedded the herd early to graze a mite, got 'em up early to do that some more, and drifted them on in along the river, watering them a heap all the way.

Of course, once they'd run all but the half dozen they'd lost on the trail into the yards of the meat packer who'd ordered them, he allowed it was too close to *siesta* time to weigh that much beef and said he'd be proud to settle up with Connie that evening, after everyone had rested up and those water-logged steers had time to sweat off a few tons under the West Texas sun.

Connie didn't argue. That was the way things went in West Texas. She'd over-watered her stock with just such bargaining in mind.

On longer trail drives with pick-up crews of extra drovers it was the custom to pay the hands off at the end of the drive. But seeing they all worked steady for the D Bar L and it wasn't the end of the month, she had Slim stand everyone a drink at the Eagle Saloon and tell them they were free to spend the rest of the coming weekend as they saw fit. So Longarm finished his needed beer and drifted off as if to take a leak, then leg it over to the Western Union on Military Plaza.

They were holding a night letter from Billy Vail for him. They'd located Greek Steve Pantages, hanging out in a pool hall in El Paso, where he seemed to be winning enough sober to get drunk more often. El Paso was awaiting their pleasure on whether to pick up Greek Steve or not. Longarm hadn't been too clear on what he wanted Greek Steve for because he hadn't been too sure when he'd sent out his query. As far as anyone could tell, Greek Steve had lit out from Sheffield-Crossing alone and didn't seem to be doing anything that awful over in El Paso. Marshal Vail had wired about for anything anyone had on that mysterious Hogan riding with Devil Dave. If Hogan had a serious record, it was likely under another name.

Longarm wired back that he didn't haven anything on Greek Steve beyond some mighty suspicious moves inspired by what seemed a guilty conscience. He suggested that as long as they knew where Greek Steve was they keep an eye on him but leave him enough rope, for now.

Leaving the Western Union in the dazzle of the late morning sun, Longarm considered a certain chambermaid who liked to be made in bed at a nearby posada. He was in desperate need of such *siesta* time after all those lonesome nights in a bedroll on the cold, cold ground.

On the other hand, the three fastest means of communication known to current science were said to be telegraph, telephone, and tell a woman. The pretty little thing was not only *Tejana* but knew he was known south of the border as *El Brazo Largo* and north of it as The Law. Swearing her to silence would be chancing too much for the possible pleasures of her company.

Meanwhile *La Siesta* was coming on and they'd be shutting down the town in his fool face if he didn't find *some* cool place to hole up for the next four hours.

A familiar voice called his name, or it called to Dunk Crawford at any rate. Longarm squinted against the glare of the almost overhead sun and made out El Moro and his two pals, Pablo and Latigo, coming out of the bank near that big Cathedral of San Fernando all the Papist quality folk went to these days, because the original mission of San Antonio de Alarcon, or The Alamo, was now a shrine to a different way of thinking.

As he strode over to them El Moro asked, "What are you looking for over here on Military Plaza, amigo? There ain't no pussy to be found at high noon, even in La Villita by the river."

Longarm said, "I noticed. I was looking for a posada to spend my *siesta* in a real bed for a change. I don't want to bed down out by the chuck wagon any sooner than I have to!"

El Moro chuckled and agreed, "*La vida del Vaquero* is no bed of *rosas*. One of these days I am going for to have my own *rancho* down in *Chihuahua* and when you all come to work for me *La Siesta* will begin an hour early with the *tequila* on me."

His pals laughed when he added, "You got to get your own woman. I would rob a bank before I would pimp. But come with us and see if you like what you see, eh?"

So they wound up in a cantina across from a more sedate posada in the Villita, or old quarter of San Antone.

It was darker inside, if not much cooler, where the air hung heavy with the mingled smells of life near the border. Longarm had been far enough south as well as north of the border to have noticed there was a sort of Anglo-Mex contest going on, with both sides bragging on how hot tamales ought to be, what proof tequila ought to be, how high a rider's boot heels ought to rise under him, and so on. It wasn't too clear why there ought to be overtones of cactus candy and corn husks in a serious drinking establishment, but he wasn't surprised.

As the four of them bellied up to the bar, without any gals at all to be seen, El Moro asked if Dunk Crawford recalled another New Mexico rider called Iago Casas.

When Longarm had to allow the name meant nothing to

him, the *Tejano* insisted, "Wiry little *mestizo*. Looks as if he could be a *muchacho* in his big brother's *vaquero* costume. He says he might know you from Fort Sumner. I told him about you saving my life and those droll arguments we shared with those Anglo townsmen along the trail, and he said you sounded like a *pistolero* he rode with a few summers ago."

Longarm truthfully replied, "I've been through Fort Sumner a time or two since the Maxwells bought it off the army and converted it to their private trail town and homespread. But I'd remember riding with a Mex who looks like a kid, no offense. I've never ridden with that Anglo runt called Billy the Kid, despite what some seem to think when you tell 'em you've rid for the Jingle Bob. What's this Iago Casas up to, here in San Antone?"

El Moro looked away and murmured, "*¿Quien sabe?* A man does what he must to get along. He said he did not want us talking about him if you were not the tall Anglo he knew in Fort Sumner, carrying his .44–40 cross-draw."

Longarm had no call to care about every tough-talking saddle tramp in the Southwest. He wasn't serious about that bounty on The Kid, if body had to brag on bad men around Fort Sumner, and he'd never heard of a want called Iago Casas.

He suppressed a yawn and asked, "Have any of you ever tried that posada across the way? I admire thick 'dobe walls and small windows when it's this hot outside."

El Moro sighed and said, "Is not for us to say what is like inside. La Patrona Consuela sometimes stays there, with her *segundo*, Gonzales. They don't pay *vaqueros pobre pero honesto* enough for to spend our *siestas* in such *lujuria*. Are you sure you don't know Iago Casas? Is a very good deal we could cut you in on, if only you were known to a man of *empresa!*"

Longarm finished his drink, set the glass on the bar upside down and said, "Never heard of him and it's going on noon. I'll see you boys back in camp when it's time to head back to the Pecos. In the meantime I aim to get out of these sweaty duds and perhaps catch me forty winks.''

El Moro dryly remarked they were all looking forward to riding as far the other way. Longarm told him to consider the bright side, adding, ''You won't have to worry as much about cow shit as you spread your bedrolls after a day in the saddle.''

Then he left to see how much they charged for a fancier flop on the other side of the street.

The motherly old Mex gal who seemed to run the posada said he could have an upstairs room overlooking the patio for four bits and seemed flattered an Anglo rider with no *puta* on his arm wanted to stay with them. As she led him up to his hired room he told her he'd heard her place was good enough for the likes of a cattle baroness and her ramrod. But the old gal never told him where Connie and Slim might be shacked up. She said they got lots of *Tejano* folk of quality but few visitors with gray eyes. Then she left him in a clean but spartan room with the bedding on the floor and a washstand in one corner to spend the next few hours as he damn well felt fit to.

He made sure of the barrel bolt on the thick oaken door, admired the fig and mimosa trees shading the patio and window shutters, and then he took off his gun rig to coil it like a snake near the head of the floor pallet with the gun grips up like a cobra's head before he hung his hat on the wall and sat down to haul off his boots.

He'd gotten down to just his shirt and jeans when there came soft tapping on the heavy door. Thinking the landlady might have fetched him extra towels or more water for the washstand's *olla*, he felt it safe to go to the door with no more than his derringer palmed down at his side as he threw the bolt and opened up.

Connie Deveruex slid through the inquisitive gap and bumped the door shut behind her with a firm horsewoman's hip as she said, ''I don't want anybody to know I'm in here.''

161

He smiled down at her uncertainly to reply, "They'll never hear it from me. But to what might I owe this honor, Miss Connie?"

She turned to throw the barrel bolt and lock herself in with him as she said, "Family trouble. The *propietaria* just told me you were staying here. She feared you might have followed me to her door. Did you know I was staying here, Dunk?"

He answered, truthfully, "Not before El Moro told me. We were in that cantina across the way and I asked what sort of posada this might be. He said it was too luxurious for poor but honest cowboys and threw in the fact that you and Slim stayed here now and again when the two of you were in San Antone."

She frowned and said, "I'll have to speak to him about that. Nobody riding for me has ever stayed anywhere with me. It's not that I'm a prude or a lesbian. It's simply not done!"

He nodded soberly and said, "Servants and enlisted men will get sort of uppity if you let 'em, ma'am. You say you're having family troubles?'

She nodded and said, "More than I can tell you, until such time as I can be sure I can *trust* you!"

Then she commenced to unbutton her blouse as she added, "I never had much respect for Irene Pantages as a businesswoman. But I'd have never thought of such an easy way to test a man with tailored gun grips if she hadn't been so forward first."

Longarm gulped and said, "Hold on, Miss Connie, are you trying to seduce me to make sure I ain't no lawman?"

She tossed her blouse aside, having no call to be ashamed of her proud tawny tits, proportioned more for appearance than size, and he had no complaints about the firm but feminine torso they sprouted out from, either, as she calmly replied, "I've thought all along you were a hired gun or maybe a bounty hunter. I once served coffee and cake to a polite but

162

impish older man called Buckshot Roberts. You knew him up in Lincoln County, of course.''

Longarm tried to converse as matter-of-factly as possible. It wasn't easy. She unbuttoned her riding skirt and let it fall to the floor around her ankles as Longarm was saying, ''Heard tell of him, ma'am. They do say he was a bounty hunter, hired by the Murphy-Dolan faction. Are you serious about this, ma'am?''

She stepped out of the skirt in nothing but her Justin boots, with spurs, dusky blond all over as she moved over to the pallet and sank down atop the covers, saying, ''They told us Buckshot Roberts killed Dick Brewer and wounded some of the other McSween riders as he went down in a thirteen-to-one gunfight. I'm not asking you to face such odds for my mother and me. But first I have to know you will never be able to testify against us in court.''

She lay back on the pallet with her eyes closed and her bared teeth clenched as she gritted, ''Come have your way with me. I don't really mind.''

Of course, and as any married-up gal could have told her, there is nothing short of throwing a bucket of ice water over a man's naked ass that could possibly discourage an erection better than a gal saying she didn't really mind, in that superior tone young boys heard, all the time they were growing up, from mothers fixing to wash their fresh mouths out with soap, or schoolmarms fixing to give them a few good licks with a ruler.

He knew Billy Vail wouldn't want him messing with her in any case. She was so right about it being mighty unwise for a man who might have to arrest a gal even staring at her turgid nipples and inviting ring-dang-doo in broad-ass daylight, like so!

On the other hand, he had seen all she had to offer, and she'd be as able to say so whether he did more than peek or not. He was still a tad undecided as he absently unbuttoned his own duds, considering how he'd likely never get her to

163

talk unless he made just a few sacrifices in the name of the law.

She'd been peeking, too, despite the way she was pretending to have her eyes closed. For as he dropped his jeans to stand over her in all his own bare glory she gaped and knocked her knees together, pleading, "Please be gentle, Dunk. I'm not pretending to be a convent girl, but I haven't had *that* much experience!"

He dropped to the pallet beside her to take her in hand, both ways, with his free hand softly strumming her Spanish guitar as their lips met for the first time.

They were both surprised by how sugar and spicy an almost innocent kiss could feel betwixt two experienced adults who'd been sleeping all alone after a day in the saddle.

So it seemed to warm her up considerable when he commenced to explore her pearly teeth with his tongue while he fingered her crotch in three-quarter time. For her thighs had suddenly been flung wide, and she reached down between them to grope for his old organ grinder.

As she grasped it, they both gasped, because she grasped good and because she'd seldom grasped anything she wanted that much.

As she guided it into position and Longarm simply settled into her love saddle to touch bottom with his raging erection and let fly the wad he'd been saving up for days, she sobbed, "Oh, no! Not so soon!"

Then she saw he had no intention of taking it out, or even stopping, and so, as he churned their mingled body juices inside her whilst she moved her hips to help, Longarm couldn't resist remarking, "I'm sure glad you're being such a sport about all this, ma'am. I know it must feel disgusting as all get-out, but you know what brutes we menfolk are to you fastidious little things."

She laughed like a mean little kid and said, "Shut up and do that faster. I'm surprised beyond words. But I seem about to come, and I'm so happy that you're going to kill that son of a bitch for me!"

Chapter 21

Connie got on top so he could nibble her nipples whilst she talked. Longarm might have felt bad about the two-faced position he was in if the position they were in hadn't felt so good.

When she asked how much he charged to kill a man, he told her he had to know who she might have in mind. So she said, "His name's Jim Hogan. He claims to be a friend of my kid brother. But would any friend blackmail your poor old mother, threatening to tell the law where her wayward son was unless she paid him to keep quiet?"

He didn't think he ought to tell her he'd be willing to make a deal with her Jim Hogan, seeing they had no outstanding warrants on anybody by that handle, once you left out the gunplay in Judge Dickerson's courtroom. He thrust his hips teasingly and asked, "How come you can't sic your high-priced law firm on the jasper?"

She clamped down with her vaginal muscles, saying, "I just told you. He told our mother he knows where David is, and he's warned her he'd be proud to tell anyone she brought in to the case. He says he has nothing to hide. It's her son the law wants to know about."

Longarm kissed a bouncing breast thoughtfully and tried, "All I know about your kid brother is what I've been told about his wild nature. But didn't somebody say this Jim Hogan was one of the gents who busted him out of some jail?''

She nodded, bounced, and replied, ''It was a federal courthouse. David was on trial for his life. They even killed a lawyer on our side and wounded another. But Jim Hogan says nobody can prove who fired at whom or whether they fired at all. I told my mother I thought he was bluffing. She's too frightened to take that chance. I don't know how much he's extorted from her, so far. I've only seen him at a distance. Each time he gets word to her and she agrees to meet with him alone he tells her that will be the last hush-money she has to give him. I have told her there is never enough money to satisfy a blackmailer and since she won't listen, I want Jim Hogan dead. It is not as if I was asking you to shoot a business rival or even a false lover. The man is a wanted outlaw. You won't get in any trouble if you kill him. They may offer you a bounty on top of mine. How much do I have to offer you to rid us of this pest?''

He'd gotten poker-hard again but resisted the impulse to roll her over and finish right in her juicy little ring-dang-doo. He said he'd have to study on that and asked where her brother might be and why he wouldn't be willing to keep the business in the family, seeing nobody was after anyone else.

She answered, simply, ''I don't know where David is. If our mother does, she refuses to tell anyone else. Not even me. I haven't been able to make her take me along when she goes to meet with Jim Hogan. David could be long gone, or my poor misguided mother could be hiding him as she has done in the past.''

He couldn't hold out any longer. So they came together with her on the bottom in a long mutual miracle, and then he felt calm enough to ask how come she thought her mother was misguided.

She kissed him, sighed, and said, ''You've surely heard what sort of man my mischievous little brother grew up to be. We've tried everything. Nobody can reason with him. I know they say blood's thicker than water, but David is just

166

plain evil! I don't know why she's the only one who's never been able to see that. But she's helped him time and time again, no matter what he's done or who he's hurt, and now she's throwing good money after bad, paying off a black-mailer with a bottomless thirst for blood money!''

He propped himself up on one elbow to twist some damp pubic hair thoughtfully as he asked why she couldn't just cut her mother's money off.

She moved his hand to a more serious position as she replied in a conversational tone, ''It's her money as much as it's mine. I run the family business because I'm best suited to the chore, not because I'm the sole owner of the D Bar L. I can't stop her from making payment after payment as long as Jim Hogan is alive. On the other hand, she'd have a time paying blackmail to a dead man, and, as I said, there may be extra bounty money posted on him. Can I get on top again?''

Without waiting for his permit she swung a tawny bare leg over him to plant a spurred boot on either side of his naked hips as she braced her hunkered weight under her center of gravity with a naked buttock almost getting spur-raked every time she squatted all the way with him as far up inside her as she went. So he didn't ask just how she meant to set the treacherous Jim Hogan up for assassination. They had a long and likely mighty pleasant ride back to Sheffield-Crossing ahead of them to work such details out. She must have been thinking along the same because once she'd pleasured herself another time that way she all of a sudden said, ''I have to get back to my own room, *Querido*. My *segundo* must not know how much I favor you, and I asked him to awaken me early this afternoon so we can meet our buyer at the bank this evening.''

He almost asked a dumb question. But it stood to reason a bank that shut down for *la Siesta* early in the day would open up again once things cooled off. He asked if she wanted him to tag along and back Slim when they were payed off, seeing they were talking about real money.

She slowly slid off his semi-erection with a dreamy smile

167

and told him, "The less others see us together, the less they may suspect us of what we might be up to. Chongo will be there with us, and we only have to take the money across Military Plaza from that meat packer's bank to my own. You did not think I meant to ride all the way home with that much *cash*, did you? My bank in Sheffield-Crossing draws on their main branch here in San Antonio to honor my checks for me. As I keep telling my poor mother, it's not safe to keep a lot of money around any house."

Longarm started to ask if the older woman wrote checks or just drew cash from their family account when she met up with that Jim Hogan. But he didn't want her daughter to wonder why he was so interested in any members of her family.

So he lit a cheroot and watched fondly as she cleaned herself up at the corner stand and dressed with a facility that made a man wonder just how often she might find herself in such situations, whether it was smart to diddle the hired help or not.

Then she was gone, just as he was warning himself to be fair and not hold a sporting horsewoman to more rigorous standards than a rider of the male persuasion.

He rolled up to lock the door after her, had himself his own whore bath at the corner stand, rubbing the soap rag that had washed her old ring-dang-doo over his own organ grinder, and lay back down to smoke and laze as it got ever hotter, and he was sort of glad he lay there in his birthday suit alone.

He caught a few winks of fitful sleep, and then he was jarred back to his senses by a rumble of thunder and sat up to enjoy the sudden cool as little wet frogs seemed to be doing a war dance in the tree branches just outside.

He got up and rubbed a damp rag over himself to peel off another layer of sweat. Then, seeing his pocket watch said it was after four in the afternoon and his stomach said it was feeling empty, he began to slowly dress while the rain came down outside and heat lightning painted the 'dobe walls chalk-white from time to time.

He figured Connie and her boys would be fixing to meet

that buyer over to Military Plaza any time, now. The banks would be opening once more and, even better, so would the swell chili joints of San Antone.

He dressed slow to give them time to catch up with him. Standing in a rain storm waiting for a chili joint to open would feel foolish as hell. He considered that cantina just across the way. You could likely see from the posada's front door whether they were open again or not.

But he didn't want to be bothered with El Moro, those two other jokers, or that Iago Casas playing big bad man from Fort Sumner.

Fort Sumner wasn't a trail town to be compared with Dodge or even Abilene before they sissied it up. There was little there but a bunch of old army buildings converted to saloons, card houses, posadas, and such, with old Pete Maxwell living in what had been the colonel's quarters back when there'd been call for an army installation there.

Once fully dressed with his hat and gun back on, Longarm moseyed out undecided and drifted down the stairs and as far as the exit to the street as he muttered, "None of Pete Maxwell's Mex *vaqueros* played a serious part in that short nasty war up Lincoln County way. To begin with, Fort Sumner and the rest of the Maxwell Grant lie a good eighty miles from Lincoln, which is why owlhoot riders, such as The Kid, spent any time there at all. That Iago squirt is likely some Mex who only heard about the famous fight betwixt our own kind, if he ain't one of them Navaho left over from the time the army had a bunch of Navaho planting peach trees around Fort Sumner.

As he stood there in the doorway, staring out to see the rain was starting to let up, he decided to wait until it quit entire. He lit another smoke and muttered, "Dumb name for a big bad bandito from the headwaters of the Pecos. Iago Casas, meaning James Houses, or perhaps you could translate *Casas* as Homes if you didn't look too Mex and had some Anglo blood you wanted to brag about."

Then, as if lightning had flashed inside his skull, Longarm

stared goggle-eyed at the damp adobe across the way to exclaim, "That's it! I ought to be sat in a corner with a dunce cap on, but they say it's better later than never, and it may be later than we think!"

He started running, splashing through puddles and paying no mind when his cheroot got put out. He was blocks from Military Plaza and feeling dumber by the minute as he ran, with the damp cheroot gripped in his bared teeth until, at last, he burst out of a side street just in time to see Connie Deveruex coming out of that bank near the big cathedral with Chongo and Slim. Slim Gonzales was the one packing the big canvas money bags.

The three of them froze in place in the last of the rain as Longarm called out, "Get back inside! Do it now!"

But they just stood there as Longarm charged across the plaza. Then El Moro and his two pals were running to join Connie and her older riders from a closer doorway, and El Moro was grinning like a shit-eating dog as he called out, "*¿Que pasa, me patrona?*"

Connie called out, "*No se!*" and Longarm wanted to kick her when she added, "*Pero ayúdame*". So the three of them ran over to cover her as Longarm slid to an awkward halt in front of them all, his sixgun drawn, to warn El Moro, "It ain't going to work. I got it figured. So where's your *compadre*, Iago? Or should I call him your mastermind?"

Slim handed a money bag to Chongo and dropped a thoughtful hand to his gun grips as he demanded, "*Que cono te pasa?* What are you up to, Crawford?"

Longarm had El Moro and his pals covered with their gun hands frozen as he snapped, "I'm working on it! A holdup works better than anything else they might have had in mind!"

El Moro protested, "*Pues . . . tu eres un vero cabron, gringo*. We buy you a drink and call you *amigo* and you pay us back by saying such rude things about us?"

Turning to his nominal boss, El Moro added, "Do you see us trying for to rob anybody, *me Patrona*? First this gringo yells at you. Then I yell for to ask what is wrong, and you order us to come and help you! How do you know it is not *he* who is out for to rob you? He is the one with the gun in his hand! He is the one who makes no sense as he yells at us about masterminds!''

Grinning at Longarm, El Moro added, ''What is a mastermind? Who are we talking about? Have you been drinking since you had that tequila with us earlier?''

Longarm told Connie and the others, ''He told me he had something good lined up. He said it all depended on whether a knock-around *hombre* who'd set it up wanted to let me in on it. He said this man of action was called Iago Casas. Add it up!''

''Add it up to what?'' asked Slim as Longarm saw to his dismay that in spite of the drizzle others were drifting over with puzzled smiles.

Worse yet, a nun had come out of the cathedral now to come their way with her cowled head held shyly down and her hands up her sleeves like a Chinese mandarin. That was all they needed with things fixing to break out in a rash of bullets any second!

He called out, ''Circle wide of this, sister! You gents with the money bags take Miss Connie back in the bank and I'll explain it all later!''

But Connie, Slim, and Chongo never moved anywhere as that blamed nun kept coming their way, as if she aimed to invite them all to the vesper mass in her cathedral. That had been what that priest back in Sheffield-Crossing had called the last services of the evening, hadn't he?

Then, as El Moro and his two sidekicks stood their ground, looking like butter wouldn't have melted in their mouths, Longarm swung the muzzle of his .44–40 to cover the innocent-looking nun, who in turn seemed to be whipping an old Merwin & Hulbert .41 out of one sleeve just as Longarm fired, point blank, to blow the nun's whimple and a gob of blood and brains away, to start the fun and games!

It was just as well the slower and not-too-bright Chongo

had that money bag in his gun hand. The quicker-thinking Slim spied the Justin boots and denim jeans under the swirling black skirts of that "nun" as the head-shot imposter landed spread eagle on the damp paving blocks with that other six-gun. So he slapped leather as El Moro and his two pals went for broke and Longarm felt free to shoot El Moro next instead of the lean- and hungry-looking *segundo!*

Connie was screaming at everybody to stop as Slim nailed the one called Pablo. Latigo yelled, *"¡Yo rendicio!"* and grabbed for the rain clouds. But it was tougher to surrender after you'd chosen to be known as "Lash" in Mex, and Slim dropped Latigo to the pavement along with his pals before Longarm could ask him not to.

A police whistle was tweeting, and, as the survivors stood there in the drizzle and drifting gunsmoke, nobody but a couple of copper badges in blue uniforms seemed to be coming any closer. But the Texas lawmen were coming fast, with drawn guns, so Longarm called out, "It's all right! I'm the law and these are the law-abiding folk! I left my own badge in Stockton, but I'm still U.S. Deputy Marshal Custis Long of the Denver District Court!"

Connie Deveruex blanched and gasped, *"Ay, Querido!* How could you?"

Longarm shrugged and said, "It wasn't all that tough, ma'am. We only done what we both thought best at the time and you wanted me to gun Jim Hogan for you. So there the rascal lies in that nun's habit he surely stole somewheres. El Moro, yonder, knew him as Iago Casas. But James Hogan means roughly the same thing if you're a Navaho breed. Hogan can be an Irish surname or the Navaho word for a *casa*, or house. I just now said old Jim thought he was a mastermind. Now look where all his slick sarcastic notions got him!"

Chapter 22

It was just as well one of the San Antone lawmen knew Longarm of old on sight. As they joined him and the others, Longarm began to reload and explain, "This lady would be Miss Connie Deveruex, owner and operator of the D Bar L on the Pecos. This here's her *segundo*, Slim, and her boss wrangler, Chongo. They were fixing to carry them two money bags across the plaza to another bank. Them three cadavers to the south rode for Miss Connie as well. They'd just helped her herd a heap of beef here to San Antone, and they wanted all the money she sold them for."

"Damn it, Dunk, I *trusted* you!" wailed the dusky blonde who fucked with her spurs on.

Longarm told the copper badges, "Them three two-faces figured she'd trust them, too. So the plan, as I see it, was for them to break cover and join Miss Connie and these honest riders as they crossed over to the far side. Neither Slim nor Chongo are sissies, and as you can see they are both wearing their own hardware. So Jim Hogan in yonder nun's habit was to circle in smiling saintly with that Merwin & Hulbert .41 to start the music, so's El Moro and them others could backshoot Miss Connie and the guns she'd invited to the party in their backs!"

The folk he'd just saved were staring owl-eyed as he con-

173

tinued with, "They couldn't have planned on leaving three witnesses who knew them on sight alive. Dead men tell no tales and so we're going to have to guess some details. But I somehow doubt our vanquished quartet meant to spend all that money here in Texas. It ain't that far to Chihuahua, and you can see they could all pass for Mex."

The cops didn't see fit to argue. It was Slim who waved his own gun muzzle at the oddly costumed corpse of Jim Hogan to demand, "How did you know? Before that sweet old nun drew from her sleeve, I mean? She'd have had the drop on me for certain!"

Chongo said, "Amen to that! Are you a naturally suspicious anti-Catholic, Dunk? I mean Deputy?"

Longarm shook his head and said, "Not hardly. But I had the natural advantage of being more curious about the trimmings of your faith than somebody raised to accept 'em without thinking much about 'em. There's this big old cathedral in Denver atop Capitol Hill, and they naturally have droves of nuns going in and out at all hours. But always in *pairs*. I mind one time I asked this Irish maid who works on Capitol Hill how come you never see a nun in public alone. She told me it was against rules set in Rome a long time ago."

It was Connie who gasped, "I knew that! I'd forgotten that! I'd seen my mother talking to a lone nun near our church in Sheffield-Crossing and . . . You mean it was . . . Jim Hogan, there?"

Longarm nodded and said, "He was wanted serious by the law in his Justins and jeans. Your priest back home said something about an altar boy and that other outlaw of Mission Indian extraction, Hernando Nana, had made himself might familiar with that same church and its grounds. The bunch of them must have been slipping in and out, dressed natural or nunnish, when the priest and his crew weren't paying attention. Rangers hardly ever search church lofts, whether they're Papists or not."

He put his gun back in its holster as he added, "We ought to be thinking about getting you and your money out of this rain and under lock and key whilst your own bank is still open, this evening, Miss Connie. I was recalling what your own priest said about vesper services that reminded me of a lone nun I'd seen with your momma, myself, and that reminded me of a pleasant sunset viewed from Capitol Hill, in good company, as a corporal's squad of nuns crossed the statehouse grounds, in pairs. So when I suddenly spied one nun alone, coming at us in this drizzle after I'd yelled at her to stay back, I didn't need a slide rule to tally the final equation. El Moro, yonder, had already told me him and his pals were planning something shady with a hard-talking cuss called Iago Casas. Miss Connie, here, had made mention of trouble with one James Hogan. So I'd already put Casas and Hogan together as I ran over to get here just in time.''

One of the copper badges stared down at the sprawled *vaqueros* to demand, ''They told you, the famous Longarm, they were planning to kill and rob the lady they rode for?''

Longarm modestly replied, ''They didn't know who I was.''

Slim laughed dryly and volunteered, ''You had to have been there. He had us all convinced he was a not-too-honest veteran of that Lincoln County War.''

''He lies like a rug!'' added Chongo, somehow not appearing too sore about that now.

Connie sobbed, ''Get me and my money out of this rain and away from this two-faced *cochino* I never wish to see again!''

Her voice dripped acid as she added, ''See Slim about any back pay you may feel you've earned for your . . . services, Deputy Long!''

But life was not to be that simple. One of the copper badge escorted Connie and her retainers over to her bank as Longarm and the other rode herd on all the bodies until other lawmen and the meat wagon from the San Antone Morgue could arrive. Then it still wasn't over.

The famous Longarm hadn't gunned four crooks alone. Slim Gonzales had shot two and both Connie and Chongo were called as witnesses, along with Longarm and an old Mex selling hot tamales across the way to the coroner's inquest that followed.

Connie Deveruex sat calmly but must have been sweating bullets when it was Longarm's turn to testify. He told the panel he'd been working undercover to see if he could catch some federal wants riding with the D Bar L. When one of the panel members pointed out that the late Jim Hogan hadn't been riding for the outfit, Longarm allowed that Hogan's plotting with El Moro, Pablo, and Latigo seemed close enough. The San Antone coroner banged the table and said, "You're out of order. You just heard everyone agree three whole riders for the D Bar L were in with a bad breed wanted for murder by the federal govenment! Get on with it, Deputy Long!"

So Longarm said, "That's about the size of it, sir. It's like that fairy tale about the three princes of Serendip by Mister Waldpole. It sometimes turns out that they send me after one crook and I catch me another."

The coroner said, "That's for certain. We've been told by other lawmen you were sent to Texas after the younger brother of Consuela Deveruex y Lopez, yonder in the front row."

Longarm was facing the other way. So he couldn't see Connie's face as he lightly replied, "I was. Like the local law and your rangers had already decided, he don't seem to have hid out worth mention at home. Jim Hogan was a bad Navaho breed we suspect of riding with Dave Deveruex and two bad Mission Apache. Apache and Navaho are close kin who talk the same Indian dialect. Albeit the three of them were passing for Mex. I can't say for certain where Devil Dave might be just now. He ain't around here, and I can't see him being in on a plot to kill and rob his own big sister."

The coroner nodded sagely and decided, "Then it's your contention we have met to declare them four fools killed lawfully as they were fixing to murder and rob Miss Deveruex

176

and leave the whereabouts of her brother, their pal, up in the air?''

Longarm shrugged and said, "I don't see him at this inquest. Do you?"

The coroner declared the inquest ended with a finding of justifiable homicide if they all knew what was good for them. So Longarm was free to go and he went.

Connie Deveruex caught up with Longarm at her cow camp on the edge of town as he was saddling the buckskin that belonged to him. He nodded but said nothing as he raised a knee to the pony's ribs and tightened the cinch. The dusky blonde glanced around as if to make sure nobody overheard as she softly demanded, "Why, Dunk? You never said a word about Jim Hogan blackmailing my mother back in Sheffield-Crossing.''

He said, "They never asked. Your momma ain't a resident of Bexar County and she surely couldn't have been in on any plot to murder you for money you were fixing to place in a bank account she shared with you. I reckon Hogan got tired of extorting said money in dribs and drabs. So he decided to grab a real fortune and retire to Old Mexico. You just heard me explaining that part in town.''

She softly said, "I did indeed. The rain's let up, the moon shines high, but the chaparral will be soaking wet and all the creeks will have risen. So where do you think you're going on that pony?"

He said, "It's my pony. I bought him for cash, and I'm free to sell him for the same, along with this saddle and bridle, come morning. Then I mean to catch me a stage coach back to El Paso and the railroad, by way of that county seat where I stored my badge, I.D., and other things that might have given me away.''

She sighed and said, "You sure had us fooled. You'll make it to El Paso long before my riders and me can hope to reach the Pecos. Where were you planning on spending the night?"

He said, "Another posada I know in town. I'm likely to feel a tad more welcome there, now."

He mounted up, ticked his hat brim to her, and wheeled his pony to ride off. But he was just rounding the stockyards in the moonlight when she overtook him on her own cordovan mare, calling, "Wait! We've still so much to talk about! What about my brother, David?"

He reined in so's they could ride side by side as he told her, "You just heard me swear under oath your kid brother wasn't there at the hearing, Miss Connie."

To which she replied, "I know. I *was* there. I was so sure you were going to drag our family name through the dirt and yet you didn't! I just don't understand you at all, Dunk!"

He said, "My friends call the real me Custis. I ain't so hard to understand. I was sent to bring your brother in, and I did wind up in shootouts with most everybody else but him. Like I told the coroner, it happens that way sometimes."

She said, "Then you're still after David. Yet you're headed for El Paso . . . ? Oh, I see, you think you'll find him *there!*"

Longarm shook his head and said, "Not hardly. But Greek Steve is hanging out in a pool hall in El Paso and I mean to have a few words with him just to satisfy my own curious nature. You were the one who asked Greek Steve to kill Jim Hogan, weren't you? I can't say either of you committed a federal offense, seeing Hogan was a federal want, but you sure scared the wits out of a poor bragging drunk, no offense. He told his cousin, Irene Pantages, you'd already had him do something awful for you. I suspect I know what it was. But don't tell me. It may be best to just let me guess."

She sighed and said, "You sure seem to be good at guessing! But I had to offer Stavros Pantages a year's pay to shoot Jim Hogan. I didn't want to ask Slim or any of my smarter hands because I didn't want them to know Hogan was blackmailing us. You've no idea what it feels like to have a kid brother hanging about with a bounty on his head! You don't know who you can trust, including your kid brother! Do you think David could have put Jim Hogan up to shaking our

178

mother down like so? David knew I wouldn't give him any more money until he agreed to see this doctor we know who treats queer notions.''

Longarm said, ''You told me your mother always gave in to her little lost lamb. I don't think Jim Hogan or the late Hernando Nana knew where their old pal, Devil Dave, might be. He may have ridden down this way with 'em after that Denver bust-out. I suspect a former altar boy at that church near your town house might have shown them hidey holes a wicked altar boy would know better than some. But your brother wouldn't have gone along with blackmail and murder when he didn't think he had to. I'm almost certain Hogan and Nana were acting on their own. So why don't we leave it at that, Miss Connie?''

She said, ''I don't want to leave it at that! I know what you're out to pull on me, again! You think I'd be willing to go back to bed with you, in spite of who you are, just to find out where you think my poor crazy brother might be hiding, right?''

He said, ''Wrong. As a matter of fact I'd made other plans for the coming evening at that other posada, Lord willing, and she ain't forgot my last visit to these parts. I ain't out to have no wicked ways with a lady who called me a swine in Spanish, no offense. I can't say I blame you for having some hard feelings about a few white lies, but I was lying in the line of duty whilst you and your momma were lying like rugs to cover up for federal wants. But, like I said, it's over and we've both got better beeswax to get on with, so . . .''

''So the hell you say!'' she blazed, spurring her mount up beside his to face him sidesaddle from his right in the moonlight as she added in apparently sincere confusion, ''I really don't know where my brother has been hiding. But since you've stopped pressing me about him you must know where he is right now!''

Longarm soberly replied, ''I have to talk to Greek Steve in El Paso on my way back to Denver before I can tell my old boss I'm *certain*. But I'm fixing to be surprised as all get-

179

out if Pantages don't tell me he was the one as switched the bodies so's the real Jesus Robles could be buried in his own churchyard with all his own kin whilst your baby brother was laid to rest where your momma wanted him, out on your own family land grant.''

Connie gasped, ''That was *David* we buried near the peach orchard he used to play in when we and the world were young and innocent? How on earth did you ever arrive at that conclusion?''

Longarm replied with a shrug, ''You come to the conclusions you have left after you've eliminated all the other ones that won't work. That's how come we call it the process of eliminating, and are you trying to tell me you didn't know who you were following to the grave that first time I admired you in Sheffield-Crossing?''

She shook her head wildly, swirling the fly tassles of her flat Spanish hat in the moonlight as she demanded to know who could have killed her mean baby brother.

Longarm considered before he decided, ''I reckon the others wanted to spare your feelings. That accounts for some otherwise dumb moves on your part. Ain't eliminating grand? I figure your momma's Father Confessor had to know because he gave me his word I'd never find your brother in this end of Texas. He eliminates as the killer because I just can't see a sweet old priest killing anybody on the sly. Had your momma turned to one of your other hands, Greek Steve wouldn't have been the one who lit out with a guilty conscience after you scared his few wits out of him by asking him to kill for you. The fact that he was too scared to take you up on your offer of a year's wages eliminates Greek Steve as a man who might have killed your baby brother. So who's left? See how that there process works, Miss Connie?''

She gasped, ''I do indeed! But I can't believe it! Our mother thought the sun rose and set in her little lost lamb! She covered for him year after year through thick and thin! She's the last person on this earth I'd ever expect to *murder* him!''

Longarm gently pointed out, "It was more like an *execution* than a murder, ma'am. Your brother was likely surprised as well, if he ever knew what hit him. The details as to how she managed when her rabid lost lamb came bleating home to her reeking of yet more blood and slaughter hardly mattered. A proud old lady done what she knew someone had to do, no matter how it hurt. Then she enlisted her priest and old Greek Steve to see both your brother and that dead *vaquero* they had on ice got buried decent, however informal."

They were approaching a fork in the cinder path to town as Longarm continued, "I reckon I buy your tale of ignorance, no offense. Had you not noticed the bank withdrawings Hogan extorted from your poor momma you'd have never tried to enlist me or Greek Steve as paid assassins. But you did, and in the end no harm was done when Greek Steve ran off, and I could say I gunned both your brother's sidekicks for another lady up Denver way who used to smile like Miss Mona Lisa. So, seeing I had no call to air your family linen at that inquest, I never did, and I reckon this is where I ought to bid you *buenoches* and be on my own way, Miss Connie."

She demurely replied in an adoring tone, "I've a better idea. Why don't we both ride on to that *other* dear little *posada* and let me show you I don't have any hard feelings toward you after all?"

Longarm had to laugh before he confessed, "That's mighty odd, once you study on it. For all of a sudden I seem to have hard feelings of my own to spare!"

Watch for

**LONGARM AND THE
VANISHING VIRGIN**

245th novel in the exciting LONGARM
series from Jove

Coming in May!